Ghosts of Kingston

From the files of the Haunted Walk

Ghosts of Kingston

From the files of the Haunted Walk

Glen Shackleton
Haunted Walks Inc.
Ottawa

 www.trafford.com

North America & international
toll-free: 1 888 232 4444 (USA & Canada)
phone: 250 383 6864 ♦ fax: 250 383 6804 ♦ email: info@trafford.com

The United Kingdom & Europe
phone: +44 (0)1865 722 113 ♦ local rate: 0845 230 9601
facsimile: +44 (0)1865 722 868 ♦ email: info.uk@trafford.com

10 9 8 7 6 5 4 3 2

Contributors

Glen Shackleton
Kirsi Rossborough
Stephanie Robinson
Craig Shackleton
Renata Smith
Jim Dean

Table of Contents

Preface 11
What are ghosts anyway? 15

Mischievous Spirits at Play 20
Haunted Inns of Kingston 24
Ghosts of Fort Henry 34
Afraid of the Dark 49
The Organist's Ghost 53
Ghosts on the Gurney: Haunted Hospitals 59
The Busy Ghosts of Bellevue House 67
Ghostly Spirits: Kingston's Haunted Pubs 75
Skeleton Park 83
The Phantom of Kingston Penitentiary 91
Spectres at School: Queen's University Ghosts 101
Elm Street Haunting 107
Deadman's Bay 113

Appendix A: A Short History of Kingston 117

Bibliography 125
Newspapers 127
Photo Credits 129

Tour Information 132

This book is dedicated to the many amazing tour guides who have brought Kingston's haunted history to life for over a decade.

Special thanks to Craig and Jacquie, who were brave enough to be the very first.

Preface

It would be an understatement to say that my tour group was surprised to see a police car pull up on the sidewalk ahead of us, lights flashing. The group trailed out behind me, about twenty or so customers in all, on the home stretch back to the tourist information office where we had begun. I was dressed all in black, with my lantern in hand, chatting and answering some questions about Skeleton Park and the other haunted spots which we had visited on our ghost tour. Two police officers got out and strolled up to the group, seemingly mystified by what they were seeing. After a brief explanation, they were relieved to see that we were not, as had been reported, a cult that had been holding a ceremony in the old cemetery (and perhaps even digging up bodies), but were in fact a group of regular people who were interested in Kingston's haunted history and were experiencing one of the very first Haunted Walks in the "Limestone City". In the end, the officers spent an uncomfortably long time asking for information about the tours, and accepted a few brochures. They came on the tour a little later that week with their families.

It was sometimes not a simple thing to be one of the first groups to offer ghost tours in Canada. We often drew puzzled stares and suspicious looks as we stood on the sidewalk with our hand-made sign, offering ghost tours every evening. We were regularly asked whether the tour was something put on by the city, a common assumption to this day. I remember one woman in particular who shouted very close to my face that no one would pay to just "walk around." There were many nights in that first summer of 1995 when we had very few customers who were brave enough to risk their evenings on something completely new.

Ghost tours have been popular for decades in the United States and in the United Kingdom (where I first experienced one), and I had an unwavering faith from the very start that a tour of Kingston's haunted history was a perfect fit. Kingston is a city which takes great pride in its local history and has an abundance of beautiful and well-preserved historical homes and public buildings. I am genuinely surprised every time I tag along with one of the tours at how beautiful the city is at night. I have been on or led the tour hundreds of times, but every time I notice something new or wonderful about the sites along the route.

It did not take long for those first few customers to tell their friends about what we were offering and encourage everyone they could to give the tours a try. We owe a great deal of our success to those first "ambassadors" for the tour who really understood what we were trying to do, and how much we cared about the interesting and often spooky history of Kingston. I never tire of running into the people who came on my tour in those first months, as they are often every bit as excited as I am about how popular the Haunted Walk has become and how much it has grown over the years.

I knew there would be a lot of work and research involved in setting up a tour that was historically accurate and informative, but still interesting enough to hold the attention of groups of people with very different interests. I knew that one of the most important keys to creating an interesting tour was to have both some truly shocking and bizarre history to relate, and some convincing and chilling ghost stories. There were some who suggested this could only be done by making things up, by spicing up the experience with exaggerated or invented accounts. It did not take us long to realize that truth is stranger than fiction. Kingston's past is filled with stories that are bizarre and shocking to us today, including those of professional grave robbers, hidden burial grounds and many tragic or funny incidents. Equally, Kingston has a very rich history of ghost stories. Although I knew very few of these stories when I first embarked on my research, I found that people were always willing to share their own experiences, and, often, to tell me about at least three other places where I should look. Many generous souls were willing to share their stories and their help. It is a difficult thing to recapture the spooky atmosphere and the chill you feel down your spine when sitting and listening to a person explaining an experience that was personally terrifying and profound to him or her. I have made every effort to share their experiences accurately, and I hope I have done them justice, both on our Haunted Walk tours and in this collection of stories.

Glen Shackleton, founder of Haunted Walks Inc.

What are ghosts anyway?
by Glen Shackleton, Director
Haunted Walks Inc.

One could easily be excused for assuming that after more than a decade of searching for evidence of the supernatural, I must have a decisive answer to this question. I have certainly spent enough time thinking about and talking about ghosts to know that the issue is not as simple as it might at first appear.

The first thing we must ask ourselves is what, specifically, we mean by "ghosts." Many of the stories we have come across certainly seem to involve supernatural events or, at the very least, events that are difficult if not impossible to explain, but ghost stories come in many different forms. When we refer to ghosts do we mean, for example, a physical manifestation of a dead person's image, a strong sense of a presence in a building, the phenomenon of objects moving without explanation, or even just a strong sense that someone we know has died? Tales of these very different phenomena are generally considered to be "ghost stories," but do they all have the same root cause, and are they all signs of the same type of paranormal activity?

The classic ghost that first comes to mind usually takes the form of a faded image or a sense of someone or something that existed in the past. A building that was occupied for many years by a strong personality or that perhaps was the scene of tragic events may well seem to hold onto an impression of its past. These types of encounters seldom seem to involve an "intelligent" spirit, or at least not one that seems to have the ability to interact with our world. Those who experience this type of encounter usually describe it as though they were seeing a past event play out, an event that may have repeated itself many times before. An example of this type of encounter would be a number of different witnesses seeing the image of a woman walking up and down the stairs at the same time every night. Are they truly seeing a ghost, or is this a reflection of some human ability to see events transpiring from the past? Perhaps we see these events with something like peripheral vision; we have some ability to sense them, but only in fleeting and unclear glimpses.

Some ghosts seem to manifest themselves in the physical world. Objects move or are thrown about a room, fires start without explanation, doors slam shut or footsteps are heard from otherwise calm and empty rooms. These encounters are rarely harmful, but are always frightening. It has been suggested that these "poltergeist" encounters may be a sign of some psychic abilities among the living people who are present when they occur, but most of the incidents that we have come across seem to have a more ghostly cause.

The most terrifying experiences are also the most uncommon. These are encounters with a seemingly intelligent presence, one that interacts with the living and our world. These spirits do not always come across as malevolent, and sometimes fall under the category of "friendly ghosts." They seem to represent the spirit of a person who was once alive, and have just as many different personalities as there are types of people—kind or cruel, helpful or harmful. My own experience is that most people who relate a story of a home that is haunted in this manner have learned to get along with their ghosts, almost as though they were members of the family. The people lose their fear once they realize that no harm is intended. Others are not so fortunate, and have experiences that most of us are grateful not to share.

The examples I have mentioned are only the most common types of ghostly encounters, but we can add to this list experiences of ghost ships and ghost animals, premonitions, and many others. There are so many different types of unexplained and ghostly encounters that it is easy to see how difficult it is to find one explanation that fits all of them. If it is impossible to explain ghosts in any simple way, is there anything we can do to find out more about them? Is there any way to prove that ghosts exist?

In recent years there has been a huge increase in the popularity of ghost investigations, and many attempts have been made to find scientific proof of the existence of ghosts. Dozens of television shows and paranormal investigation clubs have sprung up, ranging from the insightful to the ridiculous. Many make use of scientific instruments to try to find changes in temperature or magnetic fields in haunted spots, or attempt to capture ghostly activity through photographs or recorded sounds. Others, like myself, who consider themselves ghost historians, also believe that an investigation into the history of a building can provide important clues as to the possible reasons for a haunting. This focus on gathering scientific evidence has proven very valuable to understanding purported haunted sites, but it does have its limits. Critical questions are not always asked about what exactly the ghost investigator believes is being measured. A photograph filled with glowing "orbs" can often be easily explained by the presence of dust or moisture in the air, yet many internet sites would have you believe that these are indisputable proof of a gateway to another dimension. Electro-magnetic field (EMF) disruptions can most logically be tied to causes that are not supernatural. Electronic equipment and plumbing have both been known to cause EMF detectors to give false readings. In any case, where is the proof that the spirit of a dead person can cause changes in these fields? A ghost investigator must be vigilant to ensure that the gathering of large amounts of raw data does not completely replace the logical process of deduction.

This is not to say that the true skeptics are any less guilty of making too many assumptions, as they often will go to any lengths to attempt to debunk an account of paranormal activity, no matter what the evidence in its favour. It is important to take a critical look at unusual claims; simple explanations can often be found, but there are also many situations we have investigated which seem to have no easy explanation. A ghost story appears most convincing when there are a variety of types of evidence involved, as well as more than one witness. In general, I see ghost investigation as the process of amassing circumstantial evidence. The goal is not so much to prove the existence of ghosts as it is to add new information to a wonderful mystery that we may never understand.

The one thing that everyone can agree on is that ghost stories are likely to continue to fascinate us. Every culture has its own traditions of ghost stories and the supernatural. There are as many different beliefs about ghosts as there are stories, and it is possible that we may have to accept that the question "What are ghosts?" is one to which there will never be a definitive answer.

143 King St. East, now the Empire Life Insurance Building

Mischievous Spirits at Play

The building which is now home to the Empire Life Insurance Company, a grand limestone edifice at the corner of King and William Streets in Kingston, has been known to be a haunted spot since the 1980s, and we continue to hear of strange encounters within the building every year. People who have worked there have reported unusual noises and footsteps, dramatic changes in temperature, and windows opening and closing of their own accord. Others have had files disappear, only to reappear later without explanation, and computers have been known to turn themselves on and off, or display text on screen when no one has been typing. Still others have reported things being knocked off their desks, and have seen the outline of a small boy pass through desks and other furniture on his way across the room.

One of the most frightening incidents we have heard of took place in 1985, during a period when strange encounters in the building seemed to be quite common. One evening in that year, after everyone had gone home and the building had closed for the day, two men on the cleaning staff were given the job of steam-cleaning the carpet in a large hallway on the second floor. After they finished, their supervisor came up to check on their work. While all three witnesses were inspecting the carpet closely, they were surprised to see small footprints cross the floor step by step, leaving impressions in the wet carpet all the way across the room. The supervisor did not turn up for work the next day; her colleagues found a letter of resignation on her desk.

A woman who used to live across the street from the Empire Life building told us that she would often call the company to report that someone was standing in their one of their windows watching her. The company would explain that no one had been in the building at the times of these sightings.

On one occasion, we brought a tour group to a spot just outside the Empire Life building. As we started to tell our ghost story, several people in the group seemed to get very uncomfortable. The tour guide asked them what was wrong. In the group were three soldiers from Calgary, Alberta who had happened to walk by the Empire Life building earlier that day. They were a little surprised and amused to see three young boys making faces and smiling at them through one of the basement windows on the William Street side of the old building. A few moments later, the boys' expressions changed to those of fear. They appeared to be screaming in pain and there were flickering lights behind them as if there were a fire in the building. The soldiers looked away to see who might help them, and when they looked back only a moment later, they found that the boys and the fire had disappeared. When the soldiers saw our brochure, they decided to come on our tour to see if we stopped at that location. They were quite surprised by the rest of our story–especially the suggested explanation for the haunting.

The Empire Life building was built in 1853 for the Commercial Bank of the Midland District, but by the turn of the last century it was in use as the Regiopolis Boys' School. One day in 1899, three young boys who had been misbehaving were locked in a classroom to serve out their detention and punishment. At the end of the day, they were forgotten and left behind. That night, a fire broke out in the basement and all three boys were killed. Their tortured souls seem to have been forced to replay these terrible events ever since.

A view of the Rosemount Inn in the 1970's

Haunted Inns of Kingston

Kingston's Sydenham Ward, located next to the downtown core, is one of the oldest residential areas in the city. The majority of the homes in the neighborhood date back to the mid-1800s. Fortunately, many of these buildings have been maintained in their original splendour, and several have been converted into beautiful inns in which guests can experience 19th century style firsthand. What guests do not always bargain for is that they may be sharing their rooms with the home's deceased residents. Of particular note are three bed-and-breakfast inns located on Sydenham Street in the heart of the neighborhood.

The Hochelaga Inn was originally built in 1879 for John McIntyre, who was a lawyer and an in-law of Sir John A. MacDonald, Canada's first prime minister. The building has had many owners over its history, including the Bank of Montreal, who used the building in the early 1900s as a residence for their local branch manager. Hochelaga is the Iroquois name for the island of Montreal. The building was renovated and opened as a hotel in 1985.

For the first eight years that we ran tours in Kingston, we often wondered if the Hochelaga Inn could be haunted. Not only is it located in the heart of what is arguably the most haunted area in Kingston, but its 19th century Victorian architecture certainly fits the classic haunted-house image. We did not know until recently, however, that behind its magnificent façade are some truly eerie stories.

Several guests have reported seeing a blond-haired boy, about nine or ten years old, in their room. A university professor and his wife, a doctor, were staying at the Hochelaga Inn and came down to the front desk in the middle of the night, demanding to switch rooms. The doctor had woken up to the sound of a child crying, and when she opened her eyes, she found a young, blond-haired boy crying at the foot of the bed. She was very upset and woke her husband, who saw the boy as well. When they turned on the lights, the crying child disappeared.

Others have seen or heard a much younger-looking child who is also crying. On one occasion a woman woke up in the night to hear a noise in the hallway. She opened her door to see a child, looking up at her and crying. Before she could do or say anything else, she began to sense another presence in the hall, and she heard the faint sounds of a lullaby being sung by a woman's voice. The child stopped crying, and the woman was convinced that the child's mother was there, comforting him.

Many others have reported seeing the ghost of a woman in their room. An insurance company executive often stayed in the same third-floor room of the inn whenever he came to town. On one particular visit, he awoke in the middle of the night to see a woman sitting in the chair by his door. After this distressing experience repeated itself several times, he insisted on having a room on the first floor for all future visits.

One of the night clerks at the inn who worked there for over a decade had a number of haunting experiences in the building. One hot August morning, he was setting up for breakfast in the dining room, and put out a cereal rack which held three round cereal containers with plastic lids. Having finished setting up, he returned to his desk in the other room. Moments later, he heard a loud bang, and upon investigation discovered that one of the cereal lids had somehow left its container and crashed into the living room window, on the far side of the room. There was absolutely no one else around.

On another hot, humid morning, the night clerk was working at his desk when he heard something fall near the front door. He went to look, and found that a broom had fallen over. There was no breeze in the air that day and nobody was around who could have knocked the broom over, but this in itself was not too troubling. When he went to pick up the broom, however, he heard something fall near the back door and looked to see that the other broom had also fallen. The hallway suddenly became ice cold and the hairs on the back of his neck stood up. He passed it all off as a coincidence and went to the kitchen to prepare a pot of coffee. As he approached the coffee machine, he suddenly felt something shove him, and his shoulder banged against the wall. The filter basket that he had been holding flipped into the air and hit the floor, spilling coffee grounds everywhere. After taking a moment to recover, he opened a new bag of coffee and, being more careful, approached the coffee machine a second time. Once again, he felt a shove at his arm and the coffee went flying. He had a fair mess to clean up, and no explanation.

One of the strangest things ever experienced by the night clerk occurred one evening as he was showing a friend around the inn. As they were approaching the housekeeping and laundry rooms in the basement, he suddenly felt an ice-cold chill and was covered in goose bumps. It was another hot, humid evening and there was no obvious reason for such a breeze. He looked back at his friend who asked, "Did you feel that too?" The clerk replied that he had indeed felt the cold and could sense an evil presence in the area. Suddenly his friend asked, "Is there something wrong with my head?" The clerk turned to look at him and discovered that his friend's face had swelled to twice the normal size and was turning bright red. Tears were flowing out of his eyes like a running faucet and the whites of his eyes became completely blood-shot. The friend ran to a nearby washroom and flushed his face with water, after which they immediately left the building. All the way down the hall and back upstairs, they had a strong feeling that they were being followed, and as they reached the living room, two pictures simultaneously fell off the wall.

The basement seems to be the cause of much discomfort. Staff members say that their hair stands on end when they are down in the basement. On one occasion, a medium came into the building and said she sensed at least one presence. She asked to go down into the basement, but when she got downstairs she came back up almost immediately, saying that she had to leave the building. She offered no explanation, and did not return.

One block away from the Hochelaga is the Rosemount Bed and Breakfast Inn, a beautiful Tuscan-style villa with large verandahs and French windows, built in 1850 for a wealthy merchant and his family. In the 1930s, the Rosemount became known as the haunted house of Kingston. There are many possible reasons for this reputation. The house is well cared-for now, but at that time it was abandoned. In its state of disrepair, and with its dark iron fences and limestone walls, it may have sparked the imaginations of local children. There is some more recent evidence, however, that may support the claims that the building was haunted.

Many guests who have stayed here have had strange encounters. Some guests have had their radios turn on or off, while others have reported doors and windows opening and closing on their own. A woman and her mother saw a pair of slippers slide across the floor without explanation. A number of years ago, a Queen's University student was staying here with her mother in the tower room upstairs. When they returned to their room after a late dinner, they found that their belongings had been rearranged, as though someone had been searching for something. Their luggage had been moved around and their clothes were all in a mess. The student's jeans had been rolled into a ball and her shoes were found placed on the stairs, one above the other, leading up to the tower, as though someone had been walking in them and left them behind. Absolutely nothing was missing, and the owner confirmed that no one could have entered their room while they were gone. Throughout the rest of the night, they felt an eerie presence, as though someone were there in the room with them. Later in the evening, they were listening to an antique radio in their room. At exactly midnight, the radio turned itself off and they could not turn it back on. The owner confirmed that the radio was not on a timer.

A guest was checking out one morning, and turned around to see an elderly woman walking along the hallway. She had grey hair piled up on her head, and wore a blue-patterned dress and a white crocheted shawl. The guest reported that the woman looked straight at her, smiling. The guest turned away for a moment, and when she looked back the elderly woman was gone.

Over Christmas one year, one of the owners was working downstairs and heard voices and footsteps from an upstairs guest room. The Inn was closed at the time and there were no guests. The owner thought that it was possible that her partner was showing someone the building, but could not imagine why they would go in that room, as it was at that time filled with Christmas gifts and boxes. Later on she asked him about it; he said that no one had been there and that he himself had not been in the room. He explained, though, that he too had heard voices earlier and had tried to find the source outside, on the same side of the house as the room. The Rosemount Inn has a driveway sensor which he was able to see had not been triggered.

A former owner of the house told us that all of the members of his family had seen the figure of an elderly woman dressed in a white shawl, sitting in a rocking chair up on the balcony. Recently, a number of guests have had quite a shock while looking in their mirrors. Even though there is no one else in the room, in the mirror's reflection they see the figure of an elderly woman sitting in a rocking chair behind them. Another guest said that she woke up one night to find an older woman rifling through her purse. Understandably upset, the guest told the owners. Although they were certain that no one could have entered her room, this encounter did give them a clue as to who the ghost might be. They had in their possession a few items that had belonged to a Mrs. Robertson, who had lived in the house in the 1800s. The items were pieces of china, given to them by Mrs. Robertson's granddaughter. They thought that perhaps the ghost was that of Mrs. Robertson and that these might be the items that she was looking for. They put the items on display in the hallway. Shortly afterward, they found their Golden Retriever standing in the hallway barking near where the items were displayed, despite the fact that there was no one there.

One block further along Sydenham Street, at the corner of Sydenham and William Streets, is the Secret Garden Bed and Breakfast. This home was built in the Queen Anne style in 1888 for the MacKay family, who were local furriers. In 1996, the building was bought and turned into an inn, and soon after, the owners began to notice some unusual things. From the kitchen they would sometimes hear the sound of glasses clinking together many times in succession. When they approached the kitchen, they always found it completely empty. The owners thought this was very odd, but they were even more surprised when the same experience was shared by several of their relatives and guests over the following months. On one occasion, their son and his wife were actually in the kitchen itself when they heard the clinking sound coming from the counter behind them. They turned around to discover that two glasses had moved and were now sitting right next to each other.

There were other signs that the house might be haunted. The front door flew wide open in front of the owner without any noticeable cause, and, on many nights while they were attempting to go to sleep, they would distinctly hear footsteps coming up the stairs, accompanied by a swishing sound, as if the person were wearing a long gown. The footsteps would approach the owners' bedroom door and stop. Of course, when the owners opened the door, they would find no one there.

One night, their daughter-in-law awoke to someone shaking her roughly. She opened her eyes to see several dark figures standing around the bed, including two men and a woman. She tried to roll over to wake up her husband, but could not move or speak, and could only watch as one of the men reached toward her husband. He grumbled a bit and rolled over, and the three visitors disappeared just as he opened his eyes. Though he did not see the ghosts himself, he believed his wife completely, and said that he had felt a strange presence in the room just as he woke up.

On one occasion, the owners had a visitor who was very happy to see the place, as he and his father had lived there many years before while he was a student at Queen's University. Before they told him a word about their own experiences, he asked them if they had met the ghost. He told them that he and his father would often hear the clinking of glasses coming from the kitchen, and his father would hear footsteps coming up the stairs and stopping at his bedroom door, which just happened to be the same room that the owners now use as their bedroom. Until they spoke to us, the owners had kept their experiences confidential, and so it is unlikely that the visitor could have guessed their stories. The owners were certainly quite convinced that their suspicions about their home were correct.

The owners believed that the ghost might be that of a woman who once lived here. As they have gone through the process of renovating the place and making it more and more beautiful inside, they have noticed that these encounters have become less and less frequent. They got the sense that she is perhaps a friendly ghost who was simply upset at the mess and bother when they moved in.

The Secret Garden was sold in 2005, and the new owners quickly became convinced that the building had a resident ghost. Their bed-and-breakfast inn was featured on the television program Rescue Mediums as a haunted location. After a couple of years in the building, they have heard and seen enough strange things to be quite convinced that the stories may have something to them.

The one thing that is certain is that no one has ever come to any real harm in these encounters at the Hochelaga, Rosemount and Secret Garden Inns. The owners all feel that if their buildings are haunted, the ghosts generally seem to be friendly, and guests certainly need not lose any sleep over their choice of haunted accommodation.

The parade square at Fort Henry, 1885

Ghosts of Fort Henry
National Historic (and Haunted) Site

Members of the ceremonial Fort Henry Guard are well known for their hard work. Each summer, they recreate an accurate portrayal of the difficult life of a 19th century soldier for people who visit what is now the Fort Henry National Historic Site in Kingston, Ontario. It is not unusual for them to spend long hours in the Parade Square, marching in the hot sun in heavy woolen uniforms. It would be easy to forgive them the odd heat-inspired hallucination, or to write off their accounts of witnessing a ghostly image as the product of an over-active imagination. This explanation would satisfy most investigators, except for one compelling piece of evidence. The same image, in the same location, has been spotted on numerous occasions in the dim light of dawn or dusk, always by a member of the Guard on one of his or her very first shifts. In many cases they will ask a companion why a wooden structure is being built on the hill, while pointing toward the northeast slope that leads up to a wide protective ditch which surrounds the old fort. On each occasion they are met with silence and blank expressions before being told that there is nothing there. The structure, as these witnesses have described it, is a set of two tall wooden posts with a crossbeam between them, much like a narrow goal post set up for a game of soccer. What they have unknowingly managed to describe is a structure that stood in that exact location in the winter of 1838. We now know from illustrations done in that year that the northeast slope was the spot where a set of wooden gallows was built to hang a man named Nils von Schoultz.

Von Schoultz was a lesser gentleman from Finland who considered himself both a romantic and a freedom fighter. As a young man, he became involved in the revolution in Poland, and eventually his ambitions led him to the United States, where he joined an organization called the Hunter's Lodge. The Hunter's Lodge was actively recruiting Americans for a proposed invasion of Canada, in the hopes of freeing Canadians from what it saw as an oppressive British regime. Members of the Lodge believed that Canada was ripe for rebellion and that they would need only to provide the spark for thousands of Canadians to join them and fight at their side. Unfortunately, they were greatly deceived. Kingston has always been a Loyalist stronghold, so when Von Schoultz and his 200 men arrived, the town militias turned out in great numbers to fight against them. Most of Von Schoultz's men retreated back to the United States. Those who remained holed up in a windmill near Prescott from which they fought a fierce losing battle, now remembered as the "Battle of the Windmill". Nils von Schoultz was recognized as the leader of the group and was given a short military trial. In an unusual twist, his legal counsel was none other than Sir John A. MacDonald, who would later become Canada's first Prime Minister. Nils pleaded guilty and did not ask mercy for himself, but only for the men who fought under him, who in his estimation had been greatly misled by the Hunter's Lodge. Nils von Schoultz was hanged from the gallows on the northeast slope of Fort Henry Hill on December 8th, 1838.

The occasional sighting of the gallows has not been the only strange encounter that has been blamed on the active ghost of Nils von Schoultz. Many visitors and staff members claim that they are able to feel his tormented presence in one of the rooms set up as an officer's quarters. A series of rooms in the northern wing of the Lower Fort is set up to represent various aspects of an officer's life at the fort. A visitor is able to walk down the length of the corridor and view each exhibit behind a series of glass panels. The room known as Officers' Quarters #3 is specifically set up to represent the lodgings of a junior officer as they would have looked in 1867. There are many signs that something unusual is happening in that room. Members of the Guard have entered the hallway to find a rocking chair behind the glass walls of the exhibit moving back and forth as though someone were sitting in it. On several occasions, staff members have entered the hallway to find a glowing blue orb of light hovering in mid-air or sometimes floating in place above the seat of the rocking chair. According to their descriptions, it does not move or make a sound, but they are overwhelmed by the feeling of a negative presence, and feel a strong need to leave the area. Those who have been brave enough to return have found that the orb seems to have vanished, along with their uncomfortable feelings.

Most commonly, witnesses report that they are simply overwhelmed by the feeling that someone else is there in the room watching them. Before motion detectors were installed in the hallway, staff members would have to walk down its length in the dark to reach the light switches at the other end. This was, understandably, a very unnerving part of their job.

Perhaps this presence that so many witnesses have claimed to feel is the ghost of Nils von Schoultz, or perhaps there is a less obvious explanation. What is certain is that the presence continues to be felt, and always in the same location. Every year Fort Henry is host to several groups of children who stay overnight, and the fort conducts its own evening tours as part of the program. On that tour, they lead the children down the hallway and past each of the Officers' Quarters. At the end of the tour, the children are asked whether they felt anything strange along the way. Officer's Quarters #3 is not significantly different from any of the other rooms, and one would expect a wide range of answers, but every time fort staff get the same response: nearly all of the children say that they felt something strange only while standing in front of that room. Members of the Fort Henry Guard believe that this is the one and only room in the modern fort that would suit the sensibilities of a self-proclaimed gentleman like Von Shoultz, and that it may be his presence which is so often felt in that room.

The eerie encounters at Fort Henry have become so well-known that our after-hours Ghosts of the Fort tour has been running for several summers now, leading visitors on a tour of many of the most haunted locations within the old structure. Customers on our tour have experienced some of these same strange things in the Officers' Quarters, from seeing the glowing blue light to feeling a distinct and oppressive presence. In the summer of 2002, some visitors from Germany decided to take the tour. When they entered the room, their young daughter suddenly felt intensely ill, with a terrible pain in her stomach. They immediately took her out of the room to get some air. At the exact moment they crossed through the threshold of the doorway, leading away from Officers' Quarters # 3, she immediately felt better. She had no further problems for the rest of the night, and she mentioned that she felt it was something in this room that had disturbed her. Since that encounter, several customers on the tour have declined to enter the Officers' Quarters or left it very suddenly, either because they felt suddenly ill or because they were intensely frightened by something in that space.

While many believe that Nils von Shoultz is the most active ghost at Fort Henry, he is most likely not the only one. Thousands of people have lived in or passed through the fort over the years, and many have died there. What you see at Fort Henry today are the surviving remains of the second Fort Henry that was built in the 1830's. There was an earlier and much smaller fort on the site that was built during the war of 1812 to protect the naval dockyards, but there is not much left of that first fort today.

The fort was actively garrisoned by British Imperial troops until 1871, and then by Canadians up until 1890. After the troops left, the fort was abandoned for several decades, and has been used as an historic site and a museum since the 1930s, when many parts of the fort were rebuilt. To the greatest extent possible, original materials were used in the reconstruction and restoration of the buildings. It was the first military museum in the world to use costumed interpreters in an effort to bring the past to life. Today's Fort Henry Guard represents a typical 1867 regiment, and the members perform military drills and lead tours of the fort.

During the time that it was actively garrisoned, accidents were the leading cause of death at the fort. Some accidents occurred within the walls, but many more happened on the approach to the fort. In 1829, a rickety wooden bridge was built where the LaSalle Causeway now stands, joining downtown Kingston to the peninsula where Fort Henry is located. It was known as the Penny Bridge because of the toll one had to pay to cross it. Before the bridge was built, soldiers and other visitors to the fort had to cross the Cataraqui River on large, flat barges that had no railings. They were often overcrowded, especially after last call at the pubs in town. If soldiers missed the last barge of the night, they would have to rent a canoe to make the trip across the river. In either case, if they capsized, their chances of survival were not very good, as very few of them knew how to swim.

Drowning was such a common cause of death that wealthy riverfront landowners began to complain publicly about the numbers of corpses washing up on their lawns. In addition, Kingston did not have a proper morgue in those days: the practice was to float the corpses in the harbour, tied to a rope, until relatives could come and identify them. After significant public pressure, both the Penny Bridge and a small morgue called the Dead House were built.

Even if the soldiers and civilians managed to make a safe crossing, they still had to contend with the many deep and hidden ditches surrounding the fort. Dry ditches were an important part of the fortification, as they allowed a devastating amount of firepower to be unleashed on anyone foolish enough to attempt to attack on foot. The dry ditch surrounding the Lower Fort was particularly dangerous. The few enemy soldiers who might have managed to survive the 30-foot drop would have been met with gunfire from the many rifle loopholes in the walls of the ditch. To make matters worse, there are two reverse firing chambers, or underground rooms built into the outer embankment, which face onto the ditch. These chambers allowed defenders to fire rifles and canister shots at the enemy from behind. The shots would ricochet along the walls and the curved corners of the ditch, so that there was little chance of survival for anyone caught in it. Unfortunately, this clever design also proved deadly to many of those who lived or worked at the fort. Careless or unlucky men and women often fell into these deep ditches and injured themselves, sometimes fatally. There are many accounts of accidents of this sort. In 1865, Ensign Godfrey of the Royal Canadian Rifles fell into one of the ditches while escorting some "ladies" home from the fort after dark. He died shortly thereafter. In 1849, a cabman named Robinson Boyd was thrown from his vehicle to his death at the bottom of the ditch when one of the cab wheels got caught on a stone next to the bridge. Such accidents were commonplace, but they were certainly not the only ones to take place in the fort.

The biggest danger for many was the careless use of firearms or artillery. The worst and most bizarre of these accidents involved a man named Marsh, who worked as the caretaker of the fort when it stood largely empty around the turn of the last century. He was a gunner, and it was his responsibility to fire the noonday gun that once stood right next to the front gates. On this particular day, he fired off the gun as usual. He was in a hurry to get to town and he decided to save himself some time by reloading the gun right away, so that it would be all ready to fire again in the evening. Unfortunately, he did not allow enough time for the barrel of the gun to cool off before ramming home the second charge of powder. There was enough heat left to ignite the powder–and, to make matters worse, he had decided at that exact moment to look straight down the barrel. The ramrod fired directly through his head, killing him instantly.

The dry ditch surrounding the lower fort was the site of another terrible accident. In 1838, a gunner named John Smith was ramming home a cartridge into one of the big guns on the wall of the fort. He was using a paper cartridge, which had the reputation at the time of being quite dangerous. The cartridge was torn, and it ignited before he was clear. He was blown off of the inner wall and was sent flying against the outer wall. He fell down into the dry ditch, where he died six very long hours later.

Many haunted spots are found to have a tragic history, and Fort Henry is no exception. However, violent accidental deaths were not the only reason that people lost their lives to tragedy at the fort. Many simply died from the harsh conditions of living as 19th century soldiers. It was certainly no life of luxury for most of the men. To add to the mix of restless spirits who can be found there, the fort was also used as an internment camp for prisoners of war on three separate occasions–once following the 1838 rebellion, and again during each of the two World Wars. During the First World War there were about a hundred and fifty prisoners kept at the fort, including Germans, Austrians and Turks. Although deaths were not common among the prisoners, a great deal of anguish was experienced within the walls of the fort.

It is clear that, whatever their source, the ghosts of Fort Henry seem to enjoy drawing attention to themselves. In October of 1995, several tourists were vacationing in Kingston and decided to come up to visit the fort one evening, only to find that it was closed. They parked their car in the empty lot regardless and took their dogs for a walk around the outside of the building. They walked all the way around the fort, past the back parking lot, which they noticed was also empty. As they rounded the north end of the building, they were surprised to hear a huge amount of noise coming from inside. They heard the shouting voices of a dozen men or more, and they saw the flickering of several bonfires. As suddenly as all the commotion had started, it abruptly stopped. The lights faded away and the voices fell silent.

Assuming that some special event had begun since they had first arrived, they came back around to the front gate and asked the security guard what was going on. He told them truthfully that there was no one in the fort and that he had not heard a thing. In the end, the tourists left quite puzzled. They may not have known it at the time, but they were not the first or the last to hear these strange noises coming from the Lower Fort.

A number of years ago, a security guard was working the night shift and doing his rounds, when he heard the sound of voices coming from the Lower Fort. He was walking down the ramp and through the arched entry to the Lower Fort, when he heard the loud clatter of a large pane of glass breaking, coming from the area of the schoolroom, directly across the Parade Square from where he was standing. He called out that whoever it was had better come out and show themselves. He shouted into the Parade Square, "The gates are locked, you have no way out of here." After several seconds of total silence, he radioed for his partner to come and help him investigate. While both security guards stood and watched in the darkness, they heard the growing sound of several voices coming from all around the Lower Fort, accompanied again by the sound of breaking glass. At this point the guards had had enough and they called the police, who sent several officers to the scene. The large group searched the entire Lower Fort from one end to the other, but came up with nothing. They had no explanation for the noises that they had heard, nothing seemed to be broken, and no intruders were to be found. The police officers suggested that the guards take some time off, chuckled a bit to each other, and left Fort Henry.

As soon as the police officers had pulled away from the fort, the noises started up again, this time accompanied by the sound of footsteps running around the Parade Square. After much pleading on the part of the security guards, the police dispatcher did agree to have the officers return. They sent back two officers who once again searched the fort, coming up empty handed. Just as all four men were leaving the Lower Fort, passing through the entryway, they heard the very loud noise of shattering glass coming from, at most, 20 or 30 feet behind them. The police immediately drew their guns and called for back up. Before long they had searched the fort a third time, but could come up with absolutely no explanation for what they had heard. There was nowhere anyone could hide. The police recorded it as an unexplained mystery, and suggested that the men lock up the fort and go home for the night.

After taking some time off for stress leave, one of the security guards brought in a psychic to see if she could come up with any explanation. According to her assessment, there were five active spirits present in the fort. Four of them were quite friendly; but the fifth, she said, was very angry and upset and had been taking it out on the guards. This particular ghost had been disturbed by some construction that was taking place at the base of the staircase near the men's locker room. The security guard found this revelation very interesting, as the woman could not have known that the floor in that room had been torn up only a few months previously, so that fresh concrete could be poured.

At least one good historical candidate has surfaced for this "angry" ghost at Fort Henry. A man named John McAuliffe was known to have a terrible and violent temper–so bad, in fact, that it eventually led to his death. McAuliffe was a member of the 24th regiment and he was a bit of a troublemaker. He failed to show up for roll call one evening, so a couple of soldiers were sent out to find him. They discovered him wandering in downtown Kingston, and he became violent when they tried to arrest him. He cursed and yelled at them, striking one of the soldiers with a stick and then prying away his rifle. He then spun around with the bayonet in hand and stabbed the other soldier in the stomach. His victim died from the injury, and McAuliffe was sentenced to death. He was hanged at the fort in 1835. If there is an angry and violent ghost at the fort, could it be the ghost of John McAuliffe?

What about the other four ghosts? Nils Von Schoultz has already been mentioned as one of Fort Henry's displaced spirits. Poltergeist-like activity in the bakery and schoolroom have led some to believe that there may be the ghost of a young girl in those rooms, as baking pans are seen to fly from the shelves and the heavy doors will frequently slam shut and even lock on their own. Young girls living at the fort would have spent virtually all of their time in those two rooms, so it is perhaps not surprising if one has refused to leave.

A heavy-bearded officer dressed in a dark uniform has been seen through the window in one of the guardrooms by several witnesses, though little has been learned of his origin.

Voices have been heard coming from an empty area of the dry ditch, the scene of John Montgomery's miraculous escape from imprisonment at the fort after the 1838 rebellion. He and several others scaled the wall in the middle of a terrible rainstorm to avoid their date with the hangman. Perhaps he has returned to the scene of his triumph, or perhaps it may be the spirit of one of the numerous soldiers who died because of terrible accidents in that ditch.

Easily the most widely reported and convincing sighting is that of the man nicknamed the "Wandering Ghost" by tour guides and staff at Fort Henry. One reported encounter took place in the

1990s. A senior member of the Fort Henry Guard was walking through the dining rooms one night, long after the fort was closed. Part of his nightly ritual was to walk through the rooms in complete darkness to check for candles or cigarettes that had been left burning. Quite often the hair on the back of his neck would stand on end as he passed through the dark rooms. He sometimes felt as if there were someone watching him from the dark, but he became quite used to these feelings, and what happened on this particular night was completely different from anything he had experienced before. Being a member of the Fort Henry Guard, he was very accustomed to seeing people in uniform walking around the fort, so when a tall, heavily bearded man dressed in a blue bombardier's uniform passed by the window, his first reaction was to ignore him. A moment later, however, he realized that no one else should have been in the fort at that time. The security guard was still in his room, the gates were locked, and the fort had already been checked over for any stragglers. He had changed back into his civilian clothes, so it could not have been his own reflection that he had seen in the window. The uniformed man passed by the window and walked toward the outer wall. When the Guardsman went outside he discovered that the bombardier had disappeared. There was nowhere this man could have gone without being seen.

In 2001, during one of our tours of the fort, a guide was leading a group through the barracks rooms. As she passed one of the windows, she and several customers saw the shadowy figure of a man marching across the middle of the Parade Square. When they reached an open doorway only a brief moment later, they realized that he had vanished without a trace. This was certainly not the only sighting of its kind. Guards working on the ramparts have often reported seeing a man in a tattered uniform staggering around the Parade Square, looking as though he may be drunk or badly injured.

In the 1960s some senior members of the Guard were having an after-hours meeting in one of the small rooms just off the Parade Square. All three saw a uniformed man pass by the window. They did not get a good look at him, but it was clear that his uniform was disheveled and torn. Members of the Fort Henry Guard take great pride in caring for their uniforms, so when they saw this unkempt soldier, they immediately went out the door to reprimand him. They saw him entering the room next to them and followed him, only to discover that he had vanished without a trace. There were no other exits from the room.

Although it may never be possible to discover his name, there is a simple explanation that may account for his strange behaviour. In the early days of the fort, soldiers were often forced to drill on the Parade Square for hours on end in the hot sun. This was commonly used as a punishment for public drunkenness, and given how dehydrated these men were to begin with, many of them dropped dead from this treatment. A torn and messy uniform could also be the result of a drunken night out on the town or spent sleeping outdoors after the fort had closed for curfew. Perhaps Fort Henry's wandering ghost suffered this exact fate, and continues to march on the Parade Square, forever looking for a quiet place to rest.

Is Fort Henry haunted by one ghost or by many? While it is difficult to say, the countless supernatural events experienced by staff and visitors at the fort over the past 60 years make for compelling evidence that something quite extraordinary can be found at Fort Henry National Historic Site.

Afraid of the Dark
A Personal Account by Renata (Tour Guide)

Renata Smith was a tour guide and an assistant manager for the Haunted Walk in Kingston for many years, and always had a knack for telling a spooky story. None were ever quite as frightening as the true story of what happened to her as a young child:

When I was five years old, I was afraid of the dark. Now, most children of that age are afraid of the dark to some degree, but I took my fear to extremes. My walls were painted a light colour so that my room wouldn't get too dark at night, and I always slept with my door open so that I could call my mother if I were frightened. I used to lie as still as possible in my bed, wide-eyed and as silent as I could be, picturing all the scary things that I supposed lived in my room and only came out at night. Little did I know that I would be faced with a real experience that would cause me to remain afraid of the dark to this day.

One night, I woke up from a sound sleep, and was lying in the confused state between sleep and wakefulness. I could see my reflection in a mirror across the room from my bed, and I was lying looking at myself in the mirror when I realized with a tremendous jolt that there was something wrong with what I was seeing. There was another girl in the mirror! She was standing beside my bed, just next to where my head was lying on the pillow. She was wearing a long white nightgown with lace at the throat and wrists, and she had long, dark hair. She was very pale, and was looking back at me in the mirror.

Paralyzed with fear, I didn't want to turn my head to see if she was really there, so I kept watching the mirror like a television screen. She stood still beside my bed for a moment. Then, as I watched in the mirror, she reached out a pale, small hand towards the pillow where my hair was spread. Just as I was watching this unfold in the mirror, I saw out of the corner of my eye a movement towards my head from the exact spot where the girl was standing, as though there really were a hand reaching for me from the darkness.

I screamed. Immediately I could hear the sound of running footsteps as my mother woke up and came to investigate the noise. As I watched in the mirror while I was screaming, the girl in my bedroom jerked her hand back from my hair, dropped to her hands and knees, lifted up my bed skirt, and scuttled under my bed! As soon as she was no longer visible in the mirror, I tore my eyes away from it and looked to where she had been standing only a moment before. There was no sign that she had been standing beside my bed, but as I looked more closely, I saw my bed skirt floating gently back into place from where the little girl had pulled it up before crawling underneath.

A thorough search of my bedroom failed to turn up anyone hiding under my bed, and I never saw the little girl again. I have carried the memory of that night with me until now, and I will continue to think of it on nights when I can't sleep. My fear of the dark is my only souvenir of the girl with the old-fashioned nightgown and long dark hair, causing me to ensure that I can never see my reflection in a mirror while lying in bed, and inspiring me always to sleep with a nightlight nearby.

Chalmer's United Church, 1924

The Organist's Ghost

Chalmers United Church is a beautiful limestone building located on a small parcel of land bounded by Barrie, Clergy and Earl Streets, on the western edge of the Sydenham Ward. Built in 1888, the church is a designated heritage site, beloved by the people of Kingston. It is a popular spot for weddings, and few who visit the church would believe that there was anything sinister about the building.

In the 1970's, the church gained a reputation as one of Kingston's haunted spots, especially among the organists and music students from nearby Queen's University who practiced on the organ in the church's main sanctuary, often alone and late into the night. They described what they felt was an unnerving, perhaps even evil presence in Chalmers, as though someone else were in the building who wanted to do them harm. Many of these organists had played in other churches and said it was not just the feeling of being alone in a church at night; there was definitely something there that was very different. At best, this feeling made them uncomfortable: in some cases, they actually feared for their lives.

What made the process of researching this story both fascinating and thoroughly unnerving was how eerily similar the accounts were to each other. We interviewed over a dozen women in the process of this research, all of whom had played on the Chalmers organ. Many of these women had never spoken about their experiences before, and were very surprised to be asked about it. They would then go on to describe a frightening encounter very much like the examples included below. The stories these women told were so similar that they raised the hair on the back of our necks every time we heard a new account.

In one account that was very typical of these experiences, a woman was alone in the church at night, practicing at the organ, when she sensed that there was someone behind the organ watching her. She stopped playing, got up, and slowly backed away from the organ and down the aisle towards the front doors of the church. She felt whatever it was come around from behind the organ and follow her down the aisle. She could see there was no one there but had such a strong feeling of a presence that she felt she could sense exactly where it was. It drew closer and closer to her and eventually she lost her nerve. She turned and ran straight out of the front doors, not sticking around long enough to find out who or what it was. To this day, several decades later, she still hesitates to return to the church.

On another occasion, a Queen's music student was practicing at the organ in the church late into the night. The church's main organist was in another part of the building at the time, and he became very worried when he suddenly heard the student stop playing halfway through a piece. He had never had any personal encounters with the ghost at Chalmers, but he had heard the experiences of several women who played there, and he certainly believed them. He went out into the main part of the church to find that the student had backed herself up against the wall. Her arms were extended to either side as if she were pinned to the wall and she was white as a sheet. When he asked her what had happened, she said that she had been playing at the organ when she got the strange feeling that there was someone else there who wanted to do her harm. When she tried to leave, she distinctly felt whatever it was circling around her, trying to get behind her back. She did not know what it would do if it got behind her, but she knew she could not let this happen. She had backed herself against the wall and stayed there until she was found by the organist, unharmed but badly shaken.

Several different explanations have been offered as to why the church would be haunted. Some say the church is haunted simply because it is located very close to the Frontenac County Courthouse, where many prisoner hangings took place in the late 19th century. The explanation that seems most likely, however, came from an elderly member of the congregation. She had attended the church ever since she was a little girl and she remembered that when she was younger, there was an organist who played there whom she found to be quite a strange man. Whenever she was around him, she felt distinctly uncomfortable, and even long after he died she sometimes got that exact same memorable and disturbing feeling in Chalmers church. She suggested that it may be his ghost that has come to haunt his successors at the organ. So far in our research it seems that only women have had encounters with the Chalmers ghost: perhaps the old organist's ghost has a particular dislike for women, or a firmly-held belief that they should not be playing the organ in the church.

There may be something to the association between the haunting and the organ. In the 1980s, renovations were done to the organ and the area around it. After that, it was believed that the ghost had been laid to rest at last, as the tales of strange encounters ceased almost entirely. Current caretakers of the church, however, have reported that the ghost has become more active in recent years. In 1995, there was a fire in Chalmers. It was an electrical fire, thought to have started directly beneath the organ. The fire was only prevented from causing extensive damage because of a sprinkler system that had been installed in the church that very morning. This may be nothing more than strange coincidence, but considering the history of the building, who knows?

Nurses Residence, Kingston General Hospital

Ghosts on the Gurney: Haunted Hospitals

Hospitals are usually considered a place of healing, rather than a traditional haunted spot. All the same, Kingston is home to a number of old limestone hospitals that have always had ghost stories. Not only have these hospitals been the scene of many final and sometimes tragic endings, but they were also home to many caring souls who spent their entire lives, and perhaps beyond, looking after the patients there.

Kingston's Hôtel Dieu hospital, built in 1845 and founded by the Religious Hospitallers of St. Joseph, is one of Kingston's more prominent hospitals. One of the more active ghosts at Hôtel Dieu is thought to be that of a girl named Minnie, who was what was known as a "homegirl", an orphan whose Irish parents died on their way to Canada. Many such children were forced into what amounted to domestic slave labour, and Minnie did much of the cleaning and other work in exchange for a home at the hospital. Her ghost has been seen in the hospital many times.

The more famous ghost of Hôtel Dieu, however, is that of an older nun who wanders the halls, checking on patients. Many patients have reported that she has come to their bedside in the night, and only in the morning did the patients discover that no one had visited their room at all. Several members of the hospital staff have seen her as well. One woman was pushing a cart down a hallway in the hospital one night when she suddenly felt someone seize her by the shoulder and turn her around. She saw the faint image of a nun standing in front of her. Although the nun's face seemed friendly, the woman was understandably frightened by this encounter and ran off down the hall.

Another hospital employee was cleaning a part of the hospital that was under construction when she passed by a stretcher that had a neatly folded sheet on top of it. After glancing away momentarily, she looked back and was startled to see a nun dressed in a white habit sitting on the stretcher. The woman ran into a room and slammed the door behind her. After a moment she calmed down and went to check if what she saw was real. She found that the nun was gone, but so was the sheet she had seen on the stretcher. The woman says that she was certain that no one could have gotten into that part of the building without her knowledge.

The Hôtel Dieu is not the only haunted hospital in Kingston. St. Mary's of the Lake Hospital on King Street is home to some of the most convincing ghost sightings in the city. Almost all the sightings at St. Mary's of the Lake have taken place in the oldest wing of the building. Members of the hospital staff have reported all kinds of unexplained encounters. They say that often, in the old wing, the bell will ring for a nurse from rooms where no one is currently staying. Others have reported lights turning on for no reason, or have found the water taps turned on full blast in an otherwise empty room. On one occasion this even flooded an entire floor. Now, some may suggest that one of the patients may be the culprit, but all of the patients in that wing are in chronic care, and unable to get out of bed on their own.

Patients and staff have also encountered a woman all dressed in white who will sit at their bedside or put a firm hand on their shoulder, and then promptly disappear. One of the most common occurrences in this hospital, and perhaps the most frightening, happens in the middle of the night, when people in the building can distinctly hear the sound of babies crying. There are no babies at St. Mary's of the Lake, but the building was once an orphanage, and many of the residents died of childhood diseases, so this may be an explanation for some of the encounters there.

The largest hospital in Kingston is the Kingston General Hospital. The entrance to the emergency ward is said to be haunted by the ghost of a man who was killed when his Model T Ford crashed into a tree on the site. Regrettably, we have found very few details of his story, but it is commonly believed among staff that the ward is haunted.

The most interesting story related to this hospital took place across the street from the hospital on the waterfront path in the spring of 1957. A Queen's student was walking along the path near the heating plant with her boyfriend when she ran into an elderly woman whom she knew quite well from her workplace; we will call her Mrs. Grey. She was surprised to see Mrs. Grey, who had taken several months off work to care for her husband, who was dying in hospital. Mrs. Grey looked terrible and told the student that she had gone to visit her husband at Kingston General Hospital, across the street, but the elevator in Victory Wing was broken, so she could not get up to see him. The student gave what condolences she could, but ended up going on her way. Throughout the whole conversation, Mrs. Grey spoke only to the student she knew, and did not acknowledge or even look at her boyfriend.

About a week later, the student was reading a Queen's monthly magazine, when she came across an obituary for both Mrs. Grey and her husband. It said that Mrs. Grey had died three weeks earlier, which would have been two weeks before the meeting on the waterfront path. The student went to the hospital to find out what had happened, and she learned that Mrs. Grey had been to visit her husband one last time and was told that he was going to be dying quite soon. In a state of grief, she walked out of the hospital and straight into Lake Ontario, where she drowned herself. The student found out another strange fact, which was that the elevator in Victory Wing was indeed broken, but that it had only become broken since the time of Mrs. Grey's death. We can only assume that it was Mrs. Grey's ghost that was trying to visit her husband that night.

The most disturbing hospital haunting we have heard of to date involves the complex formerly known as the Kingston Psychiatric Hospital. The hospital's roots go back to 1856, when the provincial government bought a 40-acre private estate at that location known as Rockwood Villa, and converted it into an institution called the Rockwood Insane Asylum. This original building, now known as Penrose, is an impressive two-storey limestone building, with four large stone columns at its entryway. The building, with its two modern additions, is still in use today and has been the site of a number of unexplained encounters.

Rockwood was the first separate institution for the "criminally insane" in Ontario, and indeed, the first patients admitted when the facility opened in 1865 were criminals transferred from Kingston Penitentiary, just down the road. It very quickly became apparent, however, that they would also need to open their doors to non-criminal patients. The nearest facility for these patients was in Toronto, and to avoid the expense and bother of traveling, many families had resorted to having a relative named a dangerous criminal and sent to jail, whether the person had committed a crime or not, simply so that they would be admitted to Rockwood.

Psychiatric care has come a long way since the early days of Rockwood, when patients were confined to windowless cells and often bound in shackles or muffs, which held the two hands together in one boxing-glove-like device. Around the turn of the century, one common treatment was the continuous bath therapy for "excitable patients," wherein patients would be immersed in water with only their heads poking through a canvas cover for up to 12 hours at a time.

Staff at the current institution have reported feeling an overwhelming sense of despair and fear in the basement, as though they were being smothered by a heavy blanket of negative emotions. This is not too much of a surprise, because this basement area was once used to house the most difficult patients at the asylum. Patients were sometimes left locked in chains for hours at a time; the fittings for manacles can still be found on the basement walls.

Several years ago, one of the employees was working in the building late one night; he walked down the hall, rounded a corner and saw a woman holding the hand of a child, standing at the top of the stairs in the main entryway. They were wearing what the man described as period costume, and he somehow had a very distinct feeling that they were not living people. The old building was completely closed off to the public at this time, and the employee knew that the only other person in the building was his co-worker, who he knew was working in the south wing office. The only unlocked access to the building at that time was the door through the office itself, and they had not seen or heard anyone come through the doors the entire night. The employee immediately returned to the office, trembling and pale.

The most common encounter takes place in the hallways of the building's upper floors. According to staff, a stately-looking gentleman dressed in 19th century clothing has been seen patrolling the halls and checking in on patients. Many believe he fits the description of Dr. William Metcalfe, one of the early reformers of the institution. He was the man who was responsible for abolishing the use of restraints on patients. Under his tenure, Rockwood became a leader in the compassionate care of patients suffering from mental illness. Tragically, Dr. Metcalfe was murdered in 1885, at the age of 38, when patrolling the halls of the building. He was attacked and killed by a patient who was being transferred from Kingston Penitentiary, a man Dr. Metcalfe had earlier refused to keep locked up. The man got loose from his guards and stabbed the doctor with two concealed knives that had been bound together. Some believe that the spirit of Dr. Metcalfe has continued to look out for the interests of his patients at the old building ever since.

Bellevue House, home of Sir John A. MacDonald

The Busy Ghosts of Bellevue House

Located on Centre Street, just west of the Queen's University campus, is Bellevue House. Purchased by Parks Canada in 1964, it is now a national historic site and was once the home of Sir John A. MacDonald. MacDonald was a lawyer, a member of Kingston's Legislative Assembly, and Receiver General for the Province of Canada, but is, of course, best known as Canada's first Prime Minister.

The beautifully restored home was built sometime between 1838 and 1840 as an Italianate villa. Its distinctive style was unique to the city as well as to this part of the country. Every window and every doorway was meant to showcase a beautiful landscape of nature, like a picture. The L-shaped building is made out of limestone, like most of the city's buildings dating from that period, yet this is disguised by a layer of white painted stucco, adding to the Italian look. The look is completed by the fretwork eaves, balconies, green shutters, and the large central tower which is by far the house's most distinctive feature. The picture-perfect exterior is complemented by the numerous gardens that still adorn the property. The street side is bordered by an apple orchard, while the back of the property holds massive oak trees close to two hundred years old. The interior of the villa, with its seventeen Greek Revival-style rooms, is just as elegant.

The date of its construction is a bit of a mystery, as is the identity of the architect. Some say that the house was the brainchild of George Browne: he was the architect of Kingston's city hall, and of other landmark buildings like the Commercial Mart, which survives today as the S&R department store. Bellevue House was first given the nicknames "Tea Caddy Castle" and "Pekoe Pagoda" in reference to the trade of its original owner, Charles Hales, who was a grocer and merchant. The home was renamed "Bellevue House" in later years after the breathtaking view from the building's tower.

Charles Hales came from the British Isles and was part of a small but active group of Wesleyan Methodists. He moved into Bellevue in 1839 with his wife and baby daughter. When Kingston was named the capital of Canada in 1841, the Hales moved out of Bellevue for a short while and rented the property out to tenants. Many wealthier estate owners were renting out their homes to incoming government officials and making quite a lot of money in the process. In 1842, when it was announced that the capital was moving away from Kingston and would settle in Montreal instead, the Hales family moved back into Bellevue again. In the late 1840s, the villa, standing as it did on nine acres of land, with a wonderful view of Lake Ontario, was a prime piece of real estate on the outskirts of Kingston. It was this country setting that endeared it to Sir John A. MacDonald as a peaceful home for his family.

Born in Glasgow, Scotland in 1815, John A. MacDonald moved to British North America with his family when he was a young child. His father found success as a merchant in the Kingston area and was able to send John to the finest schools. At the early age of 19, John opened his first law practice, and at only

28 years old, in 1843, he was elected to the legislature of the Province of Canada, showing his first signs of political interest. Before becoming Bellevue House's most famous tenant, he had already lived in a few places in downtown Kingston. In fact, the downtown core is now sprinkled with historical plaques identifying the buildings that he occupied as either homes or law offices.

In 1848, MacDonald's law practice was doing quite well, so his family could afford the grander estate on the edge of town. His first wife, Isabella, had been very sick for a few years, and the doctors believed that the fresh country air and the breeze from the lake would do her good. In August of 1848, the MacDonald family moved into Bellevue with the hope that it would cure Isabella. Doctors would come and go on a daily basis and visit the lady of the house in her first-floor bedroom. Isabella was too weak to be constantly climbing the stairs to the master bedroom, so the morning room on the main level was converted into a bedroom when they moved in. This was quite unusual in the society of the time, but it enabled Isabella to oversee the running of the household, and receive visitors, without ever leaving her sick bed. John recounts in many of his letters how he would sit in her room and read to her, or bring her their young child so that he could play with his mother. Unfortunately, the country air did not cure John's wife. To add to his misery, John's finances became strained. His trusted law partner died, leaving John with all his personal debts. These debts were significant enough that the MacDonalds had to leave Bellevue about a year after moving in. They moved to more modest accommodations in downtown Kingston with his sisters and mother. Living with family enabled John to pursue a political career, as others could take care of his sick wife.

In 1854, he helped to create the Liberal-Conservative party and rose quickly in its ranks. Three years later he became the Premier of Upper Canada. MacDonald was knighted by Queen Victoria for his actions as one of the fathers of Confederation on the 1st of July 1867, the same day the Dominion of Canada was created and the Conservative party, led by him, came to power. For the rest of his political career and time in office, MacDonald focused on building a strong country and surmounting regional differences. He expanded the country west by bringing the province of British Columbia into Confederation, and building the transcontinental railway linking the west to the east. Despite all these accomplishments, he is better remembered in some quarters as an eccentric character and a notorious drinker. Many historians who defend MacDonald's actions point out that none of his vices was unique to him at the time. In fact, you would be quite an unusual 19th century politician if you did not drink heavily or take bribes every now and again. It is the extent, however, to which Macdonald indulged in these activities which separated him from his peers.

Sir John A.'s drinking was renowned throughout his career. Often when times got tough in Parliament he would disappear for days or even weeks at a time on a drinking binge. He was also prone to bouts of violence, and more than once he had to be physically restrained from lurching across the platform to strangle or give a beating to an opponent who had upset him. His questionable behaviour was, of course, well-known to the people who elected him: it was considered a part of his charm as a leader, and is one of the reasons he is so fondly remembered as an interesting character today.

Bellevue House is now staffed by costumed interpreters

and is a popular tourist attraction, depicting the more respectable side of Sir John A. MacDonald's life there. It offers visitors a glimpse into the life of one of Canada's founding fathers, as well as early life in Kingston–but some of the visitors to Bellevue House find they get more than they bargained for from their visit.

Over the years, staff and visitors have often reported encounters that suggest the building may be haunted. Many staff members are reluctant to be alone in the old house. Some report having seen the ghosts of a woman and child in the building, or of a man standing at the master bedroom window. Others have described feeling a presence in the room with them when no one can be seen. On many occasions, a staff member who has been cleaning the historical house has found the bed in the master bedroom disturbed. The bed is out of the reach of visitors, yet sometimes it looks as though someone has been sitting on the feather mattress, creating an indent at the edge of the bed. To add to the mystery, the security alarm often rings in the master bedroom when the whole site is empty.

One evening around closing time, a staff member heard the distinctive sound of a tatting shuttle, as if someone were tatting, an old-fashioned activity similar to crocheting. Staff members often practice this pastime in the house; however, at that moment, no one else could be found in the building.

One summer's day, a child of around three years of age had wandered off to the top floor without his parents. A short while later, he came downstairs crying and told them that he had seen a woman holding a baby in the room that was the master bedroom. She had disappeared and given him quite a scare.

A more recent experience came from a couple who were visiting the house. They were exploring opposite ends of the cellar when they both felt a sudden drop in temperature. The woman noticed that her husband was talking out loud to what looked like thin air. She asked him what he was doing and he appeared quite startled. He explained that a woman had been standing right next to him and that he had assumed it was her. He explained that the woman had disappeared the moment that his wife had spoken to him.

Many would assume this to be the ghost of Sir John A. MacDonald's wife, Isabella, and their young son. MacDonald's baby boy, named John Alexander, died in the building only one month after they had moved in. He was just one year old. Isabella's famous illness and the baby's death make them valid candidates for the haunting at Bellevue House. With financial difficulties, illness and death, their brief stay there was not a happy one. On the other hand, Isabella passed away only after they had moved out of that house. For this reason, we believe that there is a more likely candidate.

The original owner of the building, Charles Hales, suffered as much in the house as the MacDonalds did. In fact, tragedy would befall the Hales' residence in the fall of 1844, when his young son, also named Charles, died in the building at only five months old. His wife Elizabeth, whom he married in 1836, clearly grief-stricken from the loss of her child, also died there only two weeks later. The house now held painful memories for Charles Hales, so he moved out shortly thereafter. He continued to rent the house out to tenants for many years afterwards.

With all the tragedies that have occurred in that villa, Bellevue House quite clearly remains one of Kingston's more active haunted spots.

A view of the Prince George Hotel in the 1950's,
now home to several of Kingston's haunted pubs

Ghostly Spirits: Kingston's Haunted Pubs

Kingston has great night life and is known for its many excellent restaurants and pubs, a tradition which dates back to the early days of the town's settlement. In fact, Kingston has one of the highest ratios of restaurants and pubs per person in Canada.

The now-closed Scherzo Pub (previously the Wellington) on Wellington Street was said to be haunted by the ghost of a young boy. He was the son of a baker who owned the bakery that once occupied the site. It seems that, during a game, the boy was hiding in one of the huge ovens in the basement, and, after a long wait to be found, he fell asleep. When the baker started the ovens, the boy was tragically baked to death, and since that time the building has been known to be haunted.

Many of our haunted pubs are still in regular use. One of Kingston's most well-known haunts is the building at 200 Ontario Street, now occupied by the Tir Nan Og Irish Pub on the first floor, and the Prince George Hotel above. Located on the waterfront right next door to Kingston's City Hall, this charming building, with its Victorian porch and central tower, is one of the oldest in the city, having been constructed in 1809, originally as a private home. Through its early years, it served as a home to various businesses, including several saloons, warehouses, and even an oyster shop, and has operated as a hotel on and off since the 1860s.

The staff and customers of both the pub and the hotel have reported many strange things happening in the building over the years. The haunting in the hotel seems to centre on the third floor, particularly in the area of a room most recently numbered 304. Cleaning staff have seen and heard strange things on the third floor, such as lights and radios turning themselves on or off and doors slamming shut on their own. At times, the switchboard will light up as if someone is calling from an empty room on that floor. Some say they have been shaken awake by an unexplained force, and others claim to have seen the shadowy form of a woman drifting down the hallways.

One member of the cleaning staff was cleaning the rooms on the third floor one afternoon. She cleaned all of the rooms on the floor, locking each door behind her. As she came out of the last room, she was surprised to hear the locks turn in each of the doors down the length of the hall behind her, one by one. She went back to check, and, sure enough, she found that each of the doors had been unlocked. There was no one else on the floor, so she thinks that it may have been the ghost.

On another occasion, a woman was staying in a room on the third floor with her young daughter. The woman was up very late getting work done, so when it was time for bed, she told her daughter not to worry about putting her toys away. The woman woke up in the middle of the night to see her daughter playing with some toys on the floor, but quickly realized that her daughter was actually still fast asleep right beside her on the bed. She spoke to the child on the floor, who slowly turned her head, faced the woman, and then vanished, right in front of her eyes.

The strangest story ever heard by the hotel staff came at about three one morning. An older British couple who were staying in room 304 called the front desk to report that something strange was happening in their room. The couple had been sleeping in one of the two double beds in the room when they woke up to find the second double bed floating about three feet off the floor. They called down to the front desk to ask if this was normal.

The pub has had its share of encounters as well. One night, one of the managers was locking up the pub; she was the last one there, but walked into the foyer to find a rocking chair rocking on its own. Another time, she found the doors between the kitchen and pub swinging, when she knew that no one else was in the building. Both staff and patrons have reported experiencing taps on the shoulder or flicks on the back of the head without explanation. A customer spoke to a young woman in the pub one day and was afterwards asked by some friends why she had been talking to the air; her friends had not seen the young woman at all.

A bartender at the martini lounge told us that on several occasions the cash box has popped open on its own, and sometimes beer glasses smash themselves into little pieces on the floor as though they have been thrown very hard. Customers have complained that their cutlery has shot off of their plates and onto the floor. One morning the bartender opened the cigar case and found that the most expensive box of cigars was completely filled with water. The case had been locked all night and there was no water or moisture anywhere else inside it.

The building's basement is a catacomb of many small rooms, in which it is very easy to get lost. These rooms are mainly used for storage, and one is set up as a staff break room. On one occasion, a member of the staff of Tir Nan Og was in this break room when he had a very unsettling experience. He was in the room alone, but got the distinct feeling that someone was watching him. He looked behind him and saw nothing was there, but got the feeling again almost immediately. He turned around a second time; again, nothing. When he got up to leave, however, he was hit with a strong blast of freezing cold wind that hit him full in the back, travelled up and over his neck and head and blew out in front of him, raising all the hairs on the back of his neck as it passed. He knew for a fact that there were no openings to the outside in the cellar, and no way there could be a draft in the room, so he ran out of the basement and has refused to go down there ever since.

There may be a few different ghosts in the building. Two women who were self-proclaimed psychics dined in the pub one evening and said that they could see a family of four spirits sitting at a table, being served by maids. They also claimed that the ghost haunting Monte's Lounge was unhappy with the changes to the place.

Most of these experiences are attributed to one ghost in particular, thought to be the ghost of a woman named Lily Herchemer. The Herchemer family was the first family to have a business and home on the property before the hotel was built in 1809. It is believed that the youngest daughter, Lily, was having a bit of a romance with a sailor, of which, of course, her parents would not have approved. Lily would apparently hang a lantern in her window on nights when he was in harbour, to let him know when it was safe to visit. One night, Lily fell asleep at the window with her lantern lit, and a gust of wind blew it over into the room, starting a fire in which poor Lily was killed. Some people have reported seeing a glowing light in the window of room 304, and many believe that Lily remains in the building to this day, waiting for her sailor to return.

The Merchant MacLiam pub may also be a haunted spot. For a time, our own office and gift shop were housed on the second floor above the pub. Some of the staff at the pub are now convinced that the restaurant is haunted, but many of the encounters seem to be focused on the second floor. Now, it may seem to make sense that the Haunted Walk office should be haunted, but it certainly was not something we were particularly looking for in an office space.

It started simply enough. Very soon after we moved in, many of the tour guides reported feeling very uncomfortable in the office, with the sense that someone unseen was around and watching. Kirsi, the tour manager, who spent most of her time in the office, found she rarely had a day when she did not, at some point, feel that someone else was in the office with her. Some of the guides had even been known to call out "Hello?" into the seemingly empty office, when the feeling of another presence had been particularly strong.

The feeling was one thing, but at one point objects started to move on their own. One evening, one of our guides was sitting in the office, waiting for tour groups to return, when she suddenly noticed a crumpled-up paper bag move itself all the way across the desk toward the window. She moved it back, and tried to rationalize the experience as an unusual draft. A few moments later a creaking noise got her attention. Sitting on top of a cupboard just to her right was a lantern set out for decoration. She watched as the lantern's handle flipped itself over to one side and then back again.

One night Kirsi had a very vivid and strange dream. In her dream, she was standing by the office window when she heard a girl's voice say in a drawn-out voice "Saarrraaaahhh." The voice seemed to be coming from the office kitchen. Kirsi remembers the panic she felt in her dream at realizing that she needed to leave, but that to reach the office's only exit she would have to walk right past the kitchen. Just before her dream ended, she had decided that leaving through the window was a much safer option.

Now this was a dream and may mean nothing, but the evidence that the ghost may be that of a little girl and that the activity may centre on the kitchen does not end there. The sound of a girl giggling has been heard coming from the kitchen, but by far the strangest experience occurred one afternoon in the stairwell. One of our guides came in for a mid-day office shift, entered the stairwell and found that the light at the bottom of the stairs was out. The switch in the stairwell activates both the bottom and top lights and, not realizing that the bulb was burnt out and that the upstairs light was on, she flicked the switch, only to plunge the stairwell into further darkness. As soon as the light went out, she heard a girl's voice to her left clearly say "I don't like the dark", and at that same moment a flutter of unseen fingers moved up the back of her left arm. She raced up the stairs and into the office: needless to say, we made sure to replace the burnt-out bulb shortly thereafter.

Removal of gravestones from Skeleton Park in 1893

Skeleton Park

There are dozens of hidden burial grounds around Kingston, some larger than others. The largest known unmarked burial ground is next to the Kingston General Hospital. It is a mass burial mound that once contained the bodies of over 1,400 Irish immigrants who died during the typhus epidemic of 1847. Many of these bodies have been moved, but not necessarily all of them.

By far the most famous hidden burial ground in Kingston is Skeleton Park. The park is officially known as McBurney Park; it is at the north end of town, at the end of Clergy Street, three blocks north of Princess Street. Most people in Kingston know it as Skeleton Park, and for good reason. The park was originally the site of one of Kingston's earliest and largest cemeteries. The cemetery opened in 1809 and filled up quickly when epidemics of typhus and cholera swept through Kingston in the 1830s and 1840s. The cemetery was closed to burials in 1865 and was left to fall into a terrible state. People in the area let their cows wander through the cemetery and, over time, most of the gravestones were broken or knocked over. By 1893, the place was a complete mess, and city council finally decided to do something by turning the old cemetery into a city park.

The churches in Kingston, as well as many citizens, were angered by the decision and tried to stop the city from moving the bodies, but eventually agreed to support the plan on a few strict conditions. The city agreed to provide 24-hour security in the park, maintain a list of all the people who were buried there and a plan indicating the location of each known grave, plant flowers, and keep the park free of paved walkways. Sadly, these conditions do not seem to have been met. The park today is home to many paved walkways and few flowers. In addition, we have been unable to find any record that there was ever a security presence there. No complete list or plan of the graves has ever been found.

The first step in transforming the cemetery into a park was to relocate the bodies. In doing so, some unusual things were discovered. Many of the bodies had been buried only about a foot or two beneath the surface. There were likely two reasons for this, both related to the typhus epidemic of the 1840s. People believed at the time that typhus was an airborne disease, and that victims remained contagious even after death. A quick burial, without taking the time to dig further than necessary, ensured the least risk of exposure. Even aside from the fear of contagion, with the speed at which typhus swept through the city, there was probably not enough time for proper burials. This need for haste may also explain the discovery of some mass graves in the cemetery, including one containing eleven bodies.

Workers also found coffins that were completely empty, or filled with stones, no doubt the result of an unusual black market business: grave-robbing. During the late 1800s, Kingston was the centre for a ring of grave robbers known as the Resurrectionists. These were criminals who stole bodies from local graveyards and sold them to medical students at Queen's University. They would also ship them out of Kingston harbour to medical schools in Toronto, Montreal, and even as far away as New York. The problem was that medical students at the time were required to supply all of the cadavers needed for their studies. There were very few legal ways in which students could get the corpses they needed, so they would either have to steal them on their own, or buy them from professional grave-robbers. Quite often, bodies would be stolen from morgues and funeral parlours before burial. In such a case, stones would sometimes be put in the coffin to replicate the weight of the body and prevent suspicion.

The business of moving the bodies out of the cemetery was not straightforward. The city did not have enough money to move them all: families were expected to pay for the transfer and reburial of their deceased relatives. This being a cemetery for the poor, however, most families could not pay the fees. Only a few hundred bodies had been moved before the digging was cut short when the city received a formal threat from the American consul. He was concerned that unearthing the bodies of the typhus victims would spread the disease once again, and he threatened to close Kingston to American ships if the city did not stop digging up the bodies at once. Shipping was a major industry in Kingston at the time, and the city could not afford to risk its trade with the Americans, so they gave in, and no more bodies were moved. They did, however, continue with their plans to reopen the cemetery as a city park. Rather than remove the gravestones, they simply knocked them all flat, poured dirt on top of them, and sowed grass seed. They hoped that in time people would forget about the park's previous use.

Having one of Kingston's city parks also be one of its oldest cemeteries has led to a few problems over the years. In the 1950's, people in the neighbourhood were constantly chasing children out of the park at night, as it was a fad among young boys to sneak into the park with shovels and dig up skulls, to mount on the handlebars of their bicycles. Boys would also play baseball in the park, prying up old gravestones to use as bases.

The most recent problem of which we have heard came from a man who took our tour a number of years ago. He lived right next to Skeleton Park, and found out in a very unusual way that the cemetery was once much larger than the park is today. He had been having a barbecue in his backyard with a number of his friends. His dog was doing some digging in the back garden, but no one was paying it much attention. A little later on, however, when they had all sat down to dinner, the dog came running up to the table with something in its mouth. When they looked more closely, they saw that it had some bones in its mouth, which were later confirmed to be from a human hand. Needless to say, he put his house up for sale.

In the 1970s, the city ran into trouble when it tried to install playground equipment in the park. Whenever workers tried to sink a pole into the ground, they would hit either a coffin or a gravestone. It took them twice as long as they had hoped; as well, when they put in the wading pool they found several bodies. The city continues to have problems when working in the area. The Kingston Public Utilities Commission has tried on three occasions to install a new gas line along Alma Street, formerly called Cemetery Lane. On each occasion workers have hit a body, a gravestone, or a coffin. They have been forced to bring in an archaeologist, and call off the dig.

The only gravestone left standing is a monument to the first Presbyterian minister in Kingston in the park's north corner, but many of the other gravestones are still in the park, just inches beneath the surface. In some places, you can actually see the corners of gravestones poking right up out of the grass.

People have asked us for years whether there are any ghost stories related to Skeleton Park. Not long ago, two students contacted us, desperately seeking help with a problem. For several months they had been renting an apartment on Ordnance Street, one of the streets that borders Skeleton Park, and they believed that their apartment was haunted by what they described as an evil spirit. When they moved in they knew nothing about the history of Skeleton Park and the surrounding neighborhood, but they quickly found out. One of the two students had to go to a class immediately after moving in, and did not have a chance to return home until later that evening. As she was walking home, she reached the intersection of Clergy and Ordnance Streets, and was very surprised to see a large and very run-down graveyard filled with a grey mist. Having just moved in, she was generally unfamiliar with that end of town, but was certain that when she had passed by the area earlier in the day, she had seen a city park. She continued home, but the next day she asked around, thinking that she was simply mistaken about the park's location. It was only then that she became aware of the history of Skeleton Park.

It was not long before the women began to have problems in their apartment. Both women began to feel a cold chill whenever they were there alone, and at other times experienced the feeling of being trapped or boxed in. They sensed a strange presence, sometimes so strong that they believed they knew exactly where "it" was located, and on several occasions they and some visitors reported hearing the sound of a man and a woman whispering to each other very close by. They would also sometimes hear footsteps in the hallway. One of the students came home from classes one day to hear a heavy set of footsteps approaching her from down the hall. Whatever it was stopped just in front of her, stamped a foot on the floor, and then fell silent.

At times, the two students would see objects suddenly fly off shelves, and on one occasion a heavy candle centerpiece was thrown from the kitchen counter, to break on the other side of the room. When a friend came to visit, he saw the cushion on a padded chair sink downward and creak as if someone had just sat down. Another friend said she saw a blue light like a silhouette hovering in the air in the living room and felt that it was somehow watching her.

Then the dreams began. Both roommates began having dreams about an evil man fighting to take control of their bodies while they slept. Late one night, one of the girls woke up to hear the sound of her roommate choking and gagging, as if someone were strangling her to death. She jumped out of bed, opened the door and ran smack into her roommate. Her roommate had woken at the same time, and she had heard the sound of thrashing and banging against the wall, as if her friend were in a violent struggle with someone or something. Neither had been in any struggle; neither could explain the dreams.

They began asking friends to stay over at night in the hopes of keeping the spirit away, but few would stay for long. One friend saw a black form drifting down the hallway towards him in the middle of the night. He spent the rest of the night sleeping on the floor in one of the girls' bedrooms, quite afraid to leave the room. Another friend was driven away from the apartment as soon as she first came in the door. She saw a couple dressed in old-fashioned clothing standing at the top of the stairs and staring down at her silently. She did not stick around to find out who they were.

The students eventually tried to get help; they spoke to another student who claimed to be a medium and said that she was often able to contact spirits. She had never been to their house, but said that she might be able to help; so they made an appointment to meet with the woman at the apartment the next day. In the morning, she called them and cancelled. Overnight, she had met with the spirit in her dreams and he had warned her not to come near the house. She described him as a tall, imposing man with a Maritime accent, and said that he had a dominating presence, and seemed to give off an overwhelming feeling of evil. She was not willing to risk angering him further by coming to the house. This worried them, but what the students found most frightening was that the medium was able to describe their apartment in complete detail from her dream. She had never set foot in the place.

After trying many different ways to get rid of the spirit, the women decided to move out of the building and to a different part of town. We have never heard of any other ghost encounters related to the area around Skeleton Park, but we would not be surprised if more surfaced. Historians estimate that there may be up to several thousand bodies still buried beneath Skeleton Park and the surrounding area.

The Phantom of Kingston Penitentiary

Kingston is known throughout Canada as a prison city. In many cases the saying "going to Kingston" is synonymous with being sent to a federal penitentiary. This is not surprising, since the city and its surroundings are home to a total of nine correctional institutions. These days it is hard to think of the city of Kingston without considering the impact of these institutions on the economy and history of the town.

This was not always true in the history of the Limestone City. In the earliest days of settlement in this area, there was no prison to deal with crime. Most punishments were carried out in the public city markets. There would have been stocks or pillories set up, in which people who committed minor crimes could be locked up by their arms and legs, and forced to sit in the same spot for up to nine hours at a time. They wore signs around their necks naming the crime they had committed, and local farmers put out rotten fruits and vegetables for the public to throw at the criminals. Fortunately for the prisoner of the day, there was a Kingston bylaw at the time that stated that "no stones could be thrown at the prisoner". A whipping post was set up where you might receive floggings of up to 30 or 40 lashes with a particularly cruel whip called the cat-o'-nine-tails. Perhaps worst of all were the brandings that could be received on the hand or under the arm, a punishment most often given to felons and army deserters. The brandings would be done with a red-hot iron that was held for the amount of time it took the prisoner to say, "God save the King" three times. As you might expect, there were also a fair number of hangings, as there were over a hundred offences for which one could be hanged in Kingston before 1809. Locals were hanged for everything from murder to stealing a cow, and one was even hanged for forging a receipt.

Once Kingston got into the habit of building prisons, it quickly became an important specialty of the region. One of the oldest and most infamous of these prisons is located in an area of Kingston known as the Village of Portsmouth. The Provincial Penitentiary, as it was first known, has four cell blocks positioned to form a cross, linked together with a circular rotunda. This particular design was modelled after the Auburn Prison in New York State. Today it is known as the Kingston Penitentiary, and the history of this place is full of dark and gruesome deeds, especially its early days. It could easily be imagined that this place would be the home of many angry and tortured spirits.

The limestone penitentiary opened its doors to six convicts on the 1st of June 1835, and its original mandate was one that would set the tone for the dark history that would follow. This mandate prescribed a place that would not be cruel but would be "so irksome and so terrible that during [the convict's] afterlife he may dread nothing so much as a repetition of the punishment." The usual inmates at Kingston were those serving sentences of two or more years, as shorter sentences would have been served at the county jails. Some were imprisoned for very serious crimes, but many were serving time for debts their families had incurred or other seemingly minor infractions. As Kingston was a garrison city, members of the military who committed crimes would also be kept at the penitentiary.

Prisoners were stuffed into tiny cells twenty-seven inches wide and six and two-thirds feet long. This left no room to move about once the bed was lowered for the night. Apart from the bed, an inmate would only find rough blankets, a wooden chamber pot and a small folding stool in his cell. The cells received little light, and heat only from one wood stove on each floor. The meals the convicts were given were sometimes so horrible that they could not be consumed. In the earlier days of the penitentiary, inmates would often go hungry when mouldy, worm-infested bread was the only option. The hunger was worst during the summer months when the meat could not be preserved long and would often go bad. A warden admitted letting inmates under his charge eat from the pig troughs so he could get more work out of them.

The labour performed by the inmates was economically significant for the penitentiary. Every day, after breakfast, the inmates would start a twelve-hour work day quarrying limestone, used to build new wings for the penitentiary or other buildings in the city. Some would work in the prison shops, meeting outside contracts for industrial crafts. Products made at the penitentiary were sold locally and abroad, making it a somewhat profitable enterprise.

The rules inside the penitentiary were strict, and breaking them resulted in severe punishment. Inmates were forbidden to speak to each other, or even to gesture or look at each other. As a result of breaking these nearly impossible rules, many of the earliest prisoners were tortured and subjected to terrifying punishments, including floggings and long stays without light in solitary confinement. The most common punishments were three or four meals of bread and water, or confinement in the so-called Dark Cell for a few days. One inmate, James Brown, suffered so many punishments that he was eventually declared insane by doctors when he became suicidal. During his time at the penitentiary, Brown received 1002 lashes of the cat-o-nine-tails, 216 lashes of the raw-hide, and all of the other punishments that one could possibly receive at the prison.

Even the children who were kept as prisoners were not immune to the punishments carried out in the penitentiary. The youngest prisoner on record was a boy of only eight years old. As with all other convicts who would have broken the rules, he was publicly flogged for speaking out loud. Many other children of ten, twelve, fourteen or fifteen years old were severely punished in jail simply for talking, laughing or winking. In short, they were punished for acting like children.

For 99 years, women were also kept inside the walls of the Kingston Penitentiary, until a women's prison was built in 1934. They were kept separate from the men at all times, since they were considered a distraction. Just as with the male convicts or the children, the women received the same punishments for breaking the strict rules of conduct in the penitentiary. In the 1840s, one woman went insane after a long confinement in the Dark Cell. The only difference between the punishments received by the female inmates and those of the male convicts was that when a woman was flogged, her gown remained on.

In the gruesome history of the Kingston Penitentiary, the worst time to be an inmate was most likely during the reign of its first warden, Henry Smith. This brutal man believed very strongly in severe discipline. He strictly enforced the rules against speaking and gave the inmates plenty of hard labour to occupy their time. Because of the wording of the punishment regulations, Smith was permitted to resort as he wished to cruel and unusual punishment in his prison. During his most brutal year, in 1847, he noted in his reports that more than 6,000 punishments were meted out. Warden Smith's cruel punishments included sessions with the cat-o'-nine-tails in which convicts were stripped to the waist and received up to 36 lashes at once. The warden also introduced one of his own creations, known as "the box." This coffin-like wooden box would hold a punished inmate in an upright position for as long as six to nine hours. The inmate could not move inside this box and was often poked through the air hole by his keepers. At the end of his career, Smith was dismissed for mismanagement, corruption and abuse of power. His treatment of prisoners set the tone for how things would be done at the penitentiary for many years to come.

The first warden's son, Frank Smith, was no better than his father in his treatment of the convicts. He was a kitchen steward who often helped himself to the penitentiary's supplies or sold them to outsiders. He was also known to entertain himself by shooting at the prisoners with a bow and arrow, throwing potatoes at them, sticking pins in them, and spitting or throwing salt in the convicts' mouths.

Unfortunately most of what went on inside the limestone walls of Kingston Penitentiary was not publicly known. Every visitor to the site was shielded from the realities, and often had high opinions of the place. The famous British author Charles Dickens found the penitentiary to be "intelligently and humanely run." Many other individuals also visited the penitentiary since, until 1911, people could pay an admission fee to be given a tour by the guards, so that they could see the prison and gawk at the convicts. Despite the opinions of the outside world, inmates held in Kingston Penitentiary endured horrendous conditions and the corrupt administration of the prison. A few times inmates did show their discontent with the place in the form of uproars and even riots, but reform took a long time to reach the walls of the Kingston Penitentiary.

With all that has gone on inside the walls of the penitentiary, especially in its early days, it is not surprising that some particularly negative spirits may still be hanging about the place. Over the years we have heard many rumours of ghostly activity at the penitentiary. Most of these stories are difficult to substantiate, as there is a strong and understandable reluctance on the part of the guards to show any signs of weakness or fear that could be used against them in their line of work.

The most convincing ghost story we have found involving the Kingston Penitentiary was published in a local newspaper, the Kingston Daily News, in February of 1897. The caption for the article read "Was it a Ghost? Or a Convict trying to escape?"

The story began under a bright winter moon with two guards doing their rounds late one night, with an inch of snow on the ground beneath their feet. As they rounded a corner in the outer courtyard, they saw a man dressed in convicts' clothing emerging from the door of the penitentiary hospital. He crossed the courtyard from the hospital to another building. The guards immediately lowered their rifles and ordered him to halt. He paid no attention and started walking back toward the hospital. As he reached the door of the hospital, the convict turned to face them and promptly disappeared before their eyes. Terrified, the guards reported what they had seen, and for the rest of the night the whole of the prison staff on duty tried their best to resolve the mystery, but without success. The fact that they may have seen a ghost was not the only cause of their concern. What bothered them most was the fact that they recognized the disappearing man immediately as a convict named George Hewell, who had been shot and killed a year earlier by the Chief Keeper of the penitentiary.

Hewell had been serving a life sentence for his abuse of a woman. Once in jail, he was not what one would have called a model prisoner. He had tried on four separate occasions to take the lives of fellow inmates, sometimes for very little reason. On one occasion, he had tried to strangle an inmate simply for borrowing his library book.

On the fateful day when he was shot, Hewell had tried to throw another convict off a third-floor balcony. For punishment, he was confined to the isolation cell and was given light work from the tailor's shop. This task gave him access to a pair of tailor's shears, something he was able to brandish as a makeshift weapon. After Hewell had cursed and sworn all day in his cell, and had many confrontations with the guards, the guards tried to remove Hewell from his cell and bring him to a more primitive dungeon. When several guards tried to enter, he attacked them with the pair of shears, which he had hidden from sight. Faced with a violent man intent on murder, the Chief Keeper of the penitentiary was forced to shoot him at close range.

Despite the fact that he had been shot directly in the head, Hewell continued to curse and threaten the guards. It took him more than five full hours to die. The actions of the Chief Keeper were deemed justified, and to have been done in the interest of self-defence. As Hewell was dragged down the hall to the prison hospital, he swore he would come back from beyond the grave to make them pay for what they had done. With the promise of revenge made by George Hewell back in 1896, it can well be understood that no one at the penitentiary was pleased to see him return on that cold winter night.

Despite this winter sighting, it is very possible that Hewell is not the only unexplained presence roaming inside the walls of the penitentiary. A few years before the two guards had seen the vanishing Hewell in the courtyard, staff members had heard the bells in the hospital ringing mysteriously without explanation. The cause of the ringing bells was not found that night, and several guards and keepers resigned their posts, refusing to work while such strange things were going on inside Kingston Penitentiary.

Photo of Alfie Pierce, taken in Nov. 1950

Spectres at School:
Queen's University Ghosts

Established in 1841, Queen's University is an integral part of the Kingston community. Known as one of Canada's top post-secondary institutions, Queen's is the academic home of over 20,000 students, but what is less well-known is that the university campus is also home to many restless spirits.

The John Deutsch University Centre at the corner of University Avenue and Union Street was originally built as the student union building in the 1970s, and continues to be a hub of activity as the centre for the student government and a variety of student services. The centre consists of two buildings joined in the middle to form a central gathering place, and like many buildings on campus, it is a warren of halls and offices. It is also home to Alfie's, a student bar named in honour of Alfie Pierce, who was a popular character at Queen's during his life, and who may have taken up wandering the halls of the building since his death.

A woman working in the University Centre late one night in the 1970s had a very unusual encounter. She was working in the office of the Alumni Review magazine, which at the time was located on the second floor of the University Centre. She saw her door swing open and heard a set of dragging footsteps cross the room. She then watched the closet door swing open, and then shut as the footsteps entered the closet. After she got over the initial shock, she found the courage to open the closet. Inside she found an old uniform and a pair of lacrosse sticks that had belonged to Alfie Pierce, who had died many years prior to this sighting. In life, Alfie's official position at the university was as an athletic assistant, but he was most often seen dancing for the fans at the football games. After asking around, the woman found out that Alfie had gangrene in his feet before he died, and that he had had to wear a pair of large gumboots, which gave him a distinct shuffling step.

This woman was not the only one to claim to have had an encounter with Alfie. In 1975, a custodian was cleaning the floors in the building one night when he looked up to see what seemed to be Alfie, dressed in his full uniform, standing a little farther down the hallway. Alfie smiled and winked before walking straight through the wall. The custodian was later found yelling at a portrait of Alfie Pierce that he had "better not pull that kind of trick again." When Alfie died and his will was read it was found that he had written that his "spirit" would be donated to Queen's University. Perhaps his wish came true in more ways than one!

Another haunted spot on Queen's campus is the Agnes Etherington Art Centre on University Avenue. One of the largest art museums in Ontario, the Art Centre originally opened in 1957 in the red brick, Georgian-style home of Agnes Richardson Etherington, who had lived in the building for over 70 years before bequeathing it to the university. Today the museum includes a large modern addition, allowing the Centre to exhibit over 13,000 pieces in its permanent collection, but it is the original Etherington home which remains of most interest to us, as it is said to be haunted by one of the building's former owners.

All sorts of unusual things have happened in the Art Centre; people have felt a presence in the room with them, or seen the shadowy form of a woman passing through the walls. The home still contains many furnishings that belonged to the Etherington family, and on one occasion a staff member was closing up the centre for the day when she discovered that the piano was playing on its own with no one present. Upon closer inspection, she could see an indentation in the cushion of the piano bench, as though someone were sitting there. She left the building a little more quickly that night. On another night, another staff member was closing up the building, and was turning out the lights upstairs when she heard a woman's voice telling her she had forgotten one. She went back and found that indeed a lamp was still on, so she turned it off and walked back to the front doors. As she walked through three rooms of the old house, she could distinctly feel and hear someone walking just behind her, watching her in the darkness.

Just up the street from the Art Centre, and across the street from the John Deutsch University Centre, is another of the university's lesser-known haunted spots, Dunning Hall. Built in 1960, this modern stone building is the home to Queen's Department of Economics, and is a popular location for large lecture classes. Hundreds of students walk the halls of Dunning every day, but very few know of its haunted history.

In the early 1990's, a company was hired to install a new furnace and some ductwork in Dunning Hall. The workmen on the job site noticed that at the end of each day they would often find electrical cords rolled up, ladders placed against walls, and coats hung up as if someone had been tidying, but no one would admit to having done so. This continued for weeks, leaving the workmen very puzzled. An explanation was never found and this would not be the only strange experience that they would encounter while on the job.

One afternoon the site foreman was in the men's room when he distinctly felt someone tapping him on the shoulder. He knew he was the only person in the room and quickly fled, never to return to that particular room again. Shortly after, this same man arrived at work early one morning to prepare for the day. As soon as he placed the key in the locked door, he heard an odd noise that reminded him of the sound of an air tool. Knowing that none of the workers had arrived yet, he was perplexed by the noise, which continued to grow louder as he walked down the hall. Carrying his plans and paperwork in his arms, he walked through the building, following the noise and looking for its source. He rounded a corner and saw before him a woman whose feet were not touching the ground. She spotted him at the same time, and came rushing towards him at great speed, passing by him and disappearing. The blast of wind that travelled with the woman was strong enough to pull the shirt out of the foreman's pants and send his plans and paperwork swirling. The company completed its work in Dunning Hall, but this particular foreman never returned to the building. We have yet to find any clues to the identity of this woman, or the reasons why she may be haunting Dunning Hall.

The ghosts of Queen's do not restrict themselves to the main campus. The Donald Gordon Centre, a meeting and conference facility owned by Queen's and located on Union Street just west of the main campus, has many reports of ghostly happenings. The centre's main building is an elegant limestone home built in 1841, originally a country estate known as Roselawn. People who work there say that they often hear footsteps going up and down the stairs, and some say that they have felt a presence, sometimes malevolent, in the building. Late one night in the 1970s, a woman was working in the building when she saw an elderly gentleman standing at the foot of the stairs, dressed in a grey suit with spats and a pocket watch. She said he had grey and white hair but was balding, and was clean shaven. Thinking he might be lost, she asked if she could help him: he just looked at her and smiled, and then walked up the stairs. She followed him up the stairs to a room that used to be the master bedroom of the estate, only to find that he had simply disappeared.

There are two theories as to who this ghost may be. Some say that it is the ghost of a judge who once lived in an earlier home on the property. In 1788, he passed sentenced on the first man to hang in Upper Canada, for the alleged theft of a gold watch, only to find out later that the man was innocent. It is said that the judge never rested easy again. Others believe that the ghost moved in from a neighbouring house, Calderwood House, when it was torn down in 1969. Built in 1848, Calderwood House was once the home of the Canadian author Robertson Davies. Many "reputable and well-known people" reported seeing a ghost in evening dress in the house, including Robertson Davies himself. That ghost was said to be the spirit of a doctor who had drowned his two daughters in the bathtub because, he said, they were "spiteful little girls who never followed his orders." Whoever it may be, the ghost of the Donald Gordon Centre is said to make most of its appearances late at night, and usually at the end of the month.

Elm Street Haunting
A Personal Account by Craig (Tour Guide)

Aside from being among the first to conduct tours for the Haunted Walk in Kingston, Craig Shackleton could occasionally be convinced to tell his own ghost story. He was always reluctant to tell this story, as the memory of his encounter in a Kingston apartment is disturbing to him even today, but we find it to be one of the most chilling stories we have come across:

I have always found it ironic that I suffered from strange and mysterious nightmares while I lived in an apartment on Elm Street. People often laugh when I tell them that, but I still don't find it funny. Even now, almost twenty years later, every time I relate this story, it frightens me. It was absolutely the most terrifying experience of my life.

In the fall of 1989, I moved to Kingston. I had taken some time off after high school to figure out what I wanted to do with myself, and was considering going to college or university in the city. I got a crummy little apartment and a crummy little job, and was living on a shoestring budget. One of my co-workers mentioned that her roommate was moving out and that she was looking for someone else to move in. It was a nicer place than I had on my own, and cheaper as well, so I jumped at the opportunity.

For the first little while nothing seemed unusual. As I was working a lot and often out with friends, I was only home to eat and sleep, and sometimes not even that. I hadn't been there long when my roommate decided to move out. I took over the lease and invited a male co-worker of mine to move in. That was when everything changed.

The first night after my original roommate was gone, I had difficulty sleeping. At one point I woke up suddenly, as though from a bad dream. I was scared and confused. It felt like it should be morning, but it was still dark. I couldn't see my clock, so I sat up to find my glasses.

At least, I tried to sit up, but found I couldn't move. I was suddenly choking and couldn't get a good breath. My arms and legs started twitching violently. I thought I was going to black out. And then I woke up. I realized that I had been dreaming. Now I was awake. I was a little freaked out, but relieved that it had only been a nightmare. It was still dark. I looked at my clock, but couldn't make out the numbers. I sat up to find my glasses…and felt my neck constrict. I was choking again, and as before, I couldn't move, or at least couldn't control my movement. My whole body was shuddering and shaking, and I was running out of air. Just as I thought I was going to black out, I woke up.

Again. In my dark room.

This continued all night. The fifth time I woke up, I managed to drag my shaking body over to the light switch and turn it on, only to wake up in my bed again. I lost count after that, but another time I again made it to the light switch, only to wake up in my bed in the dark again. When I later made it to my light switch for the third time, I decided to try something else. I staggered down the hall into the kitchen. I was surprised to see someone standing there. He was wearing indistinct black garments, possibly a cloak. He had his hood up, and he was facing away from me. I didn't know who this could be, but I knew it wasn't my roommate. Slowly he turned to face me. His face was pale and vague, just dark spots for eyes and a mouth, like the character in Edvard Munsch's famous painting Scream. What really frightened me though was that his head was tilted at an impossible angle, his neck clearly broken. And yet he was looking at me. And then I woke up in my bed, in the dark.

For the rest of the night, I continued to 'wake up' and then find myself paralyzed and choking as soon as I tried to move. I don't know how long it went on for, but to me, it was an eternity. I did not manage to get out of my bed again in any of these dreams of waking. Finally, I woke up with the sun streaming in on me, able to move and breathe. I was exhausted, stiff, sore, and soaked in sweat. But at least I was awake. I went out into my living room. My roommate was there, sitting and having a cigarette. He was pale and shaking.

"Wait 'til I tell you about the dream I just had", I said.

"No, you listen to the dream I just had!" was his answer.

And then he told me in great detail how he had dreamed that he had woken up. He was in his bed, but someone was choking him, and he couldn't get up. It felt like there was a rope around his neck holding him down. Just when he was about to black out, he would wake up again, over and over. He never managed to get up, but in one of the dreams, he looked over to see a man in a dark cloak hanging from rope tied to the ceiling light. His neck was bent over sideways by the noose, clearly broken, but the man was looking directly at him. His face was pale and indistinct.

We only stayed in that apartment for a few months. We never had so severe an experience again, but we both continued to be plagued by bad dreams. We often felt like there was someone there, watching us, not a casual observer, but someone staring hatefully at us. Friends who came over sometimes had similar experiences, but we started to notice that it never happened to women, or even while women were present.

On one occasion we arranged to go out with a friend. We gave him a key to our place so he could let himself in, as he would be done his class before either of us got home from work. Once we were all home, we were planning to eat a quick dinner and then head to the bar. When I got home, our friend was sitting on the couch, pale and scared, with his jacket on. As soon as I opened the door, he said, "Let's go." He made it very clear he did not want to stick around for a single minute more, so we wrote a note to my roommate and went to a restaurant. At dinner my frightened friend told me, "I don't know what it is about your place, but it totally freaked me out."

Then one day, a female friend of ours told us she thought our apartment was haunted. She said sometimes she felt like someone was watching her at our place. She reassured us that we shouldn't worry; she always felt that it was like someone was watching over her, protecting her. When we told her about the things that had happened to us, she got pretty upset. She told us we should move out.

We broke our lease as soon as we could find a new place. Our landlord was unhappy, but we didn't care. We were glad never to see the place again.

A year and a half later, I was taking a break between classes at college. I was hanging out with some classmates when I overheard a girl talking about her boyfriend. "I don't know what his problem is. He doesn't like to come over, and he'll never wait there for me if I'm not there. He says he doesn't like the apartment, that it scares him, but I don't know why, I always feel really safe there. I think there's something wrong, maybe he doesn't want to go out with me...."

I interrupted her. "I bet I know where you live."

I told her the address of my old apartment.

I was right.

An early view of Cathcart Tower on Cedar Island

Deadman's Bay

On the eastern side of Point Henry where the fort stands today lies a body of water with a gruesome name: Deadman's Bay. Across the bay is Cedar Island, which is now part of the St. Lawrence Islands National Park. It is a popular camping spot today, but once played a role in one of the most dramatic events in Kingston's history. The island is relatively small and features three camp sites as well as one of Kingston's famous round Martello towers, named the Cathcart Tower.

A number of years ago, two couples were camping there. It was a pleasant summer day and they were pleased to see that they were the only campers on the island. Not long after they arrived they pitched their tents and made camp. One couple camped right next to the path closest to the docks, while the other couple was a little more adventurous, and decided to pitch their tent closer to the tower, right on the edge of a steep bank overlooking the water. The woman who had camped next to the path woke up in the middle of the night to hear a terrible storm raging outside. Despite the heavy rain, she felt the call of nature and had no choice but to venture out into the pouring rain. When she walked up the path a little way, she was surprised to see what she assumed was the other couple far ahead of her, walking toward the tower hand in hand. She noticed that they were dressed in strange, old-fashioned-looking clothing that she had never seen before. She called out to them, but they didn't answer her. Each time she rounded a bend they appeared to be farther away and she decided to give up and head back to the shelter of her tent. When she returned she woke up her partner and told him what had happened. They decided that they would ask about it in the morning, and they went back to sleep.

The next morning, they asked the other couple why they had been out in such terrible weather. The other couple said that first of all, they had not left their tent all night, and secondly, it had not rained a drop that night. Both couples checked around the campsite and found that everything was completely dry, including the clothing the woman had worn the night before. They felt certain that they had witnessed something supernatural. When they got back to town, they decided to look into the history of Cedar Island, to see if they could find an explanation for this frightening encounter.

Deadman's Bay was given its name because of a terrible accident that occurred in 1846. The events of September 12th of that year led to one of Kingston's worst maritime tragedies. Twenty-three men, mostly Scottish stone masons, were working on the construction of the Cathcart Tower. The tower was part of a network of defences being built around Kingston at the time. Three other Martello towers still stand today as Fort Frederick, Shoal Tower and Murney Tower. This style of fortification was widely used by British forces from the time of the Napoleonic Wars onward. The inspiration for these towers came from a group of round fortresses found on Mortella Point, in Corsica, Italy. Since the British were so impressed by the strength of these towers, they quickly adopted the design for use throughout the empire. With the threat of American invasion at the time, these towers were being built in Kingston as quickly as possible.

On the 12th of September 1846, the stone masons had been working on the tower a little later than usual. They could see a storm brewing in the distance, but they decided to stay and try to finish the last of their work before heading home for the weekend. The storm moved in much more quickly than expected. They did not want to be stranded overnight and so decided, unwisely, to pile all twenty-three men into a small boat and row for the mainland. The boat was built to hold no more than twelve men, and progress was slow in the choppy waters. They rowed for shore as quickly as they could, but only made it halfway across the bay when the storm hit with full force. After being hit by one drenching wave, several men stood up in the boat. The small boat capsized, sending all of the men overboard into the stormy, cold waters of the bay. Seventeen of the twenty-three men drowned on that day before the storm finally ended. Most of the bodies were recovered the next day. In the end it was determined that seventy-two children had been left fatherless. One of the men who drowned was a man named Robert James. He was engaged to a girl named Elizabeth, the daughter of the owner of the British American Hotel in Kingston. When news came of Robert's death, she was devastated. She refused to believe that he had died. She would not eat or sleep: every night she walked down to the point facing Cedar Island, and waded up to her waist in the cold water of the lake, gazing out into the darkness and watching for her sweetheart's return. Before long her health began to fail, and she died soon afterwards. We hope and believe that the ghosts of Robert and Elizabeth have found each other again, in the enchanted woods of Cedar Island.

Appendix A:
A Brief History of Kingston

One of the oldest cities in central Canada, Kingston has a rich and colourful history that dates back many centuries. Before any European settlement, the area we now call Kingston was inhabited by many native peoples. It was never a permanent native settlement, but the area was considered a part of Iroquois territory. The nomadic Mississauga people also regularly passed through the area.

The first Europeans to explore this region were the French. It was in 1673 that Louis de Buade, Count de Frontenac and Governor General of the French colony, set up a trading post and a fort at this location. The fort was named Fort Frontenac and was set up to oversee the fur trade in the area, and to play a defensive military role. Along with the fortifications, there was a very limited settlement, with some agricultural activities. The construction of Fort Frontenac marked the beginnings of almost a century of French occupation and control of the area.

After a period of peace with the Iroquois, hostilities were renewed in 1689. The commander of the fort retreated to Montreal, and Fort Frontenac was abandoned. The fort was also destroyed at that time: it was argued that destroying it was a lot better than having the enemy take it–or, even worse, having the British occupy it. In 1695, however, the French changed their minds and came back to the Kingston region. They rebuilt Fort

Frontenac and re-established their military presence. Peace with the Iroquois came in 1701, when a treaty was negotiated with the French. In following years, the fort represented only a small element in the series of fortifications along the French-British military border, and by 1758 only a skeleton force was left at Fort Frontenac. This situation gave the British a perfect opportunity to take the fort. In the month of August of that same year, Lieutenant-Colonel John Bradstreet landed in Kingston, and successfully laid siege to the fort from higher ground. The British destroyed most of the settlement as well as the fort itself. The French were sent on their way and Fort Frontenac was abandoned for good.

In 1763, with the end of the Seven Years War in Europe and the signing of the Treaty of Paris, the whole of New France fell into the hands of the British, and the Kingston region became part of Quebec in the colony of British North America. New settlement came in 1783, as the Kingston site was selected as a permanent home for the many displaced loyalists at the conclusion of the American War of Independence. During and after this war, many Americans stayed loyal to the British crown, and, fearing persecution, moved north to British North America. It is estimated that 80,000 to 100,000 Loyalists left the United States, and of that number approximately 7,500 came to what is now the province of Ontario. On the same site, the British also established a naval base. In 1791, the Constitutional Act established the two provinces of Upper and Lower Canada, and Kingston became an important city in the new province of Upper Canada.

Being located at the intersection of three major waterways (Lake Ontario, St. Lawrence River and the Cataraqui River), the Loyalist settlement quickly took on an important economic role.

Many shipping companies made handsome profits by transferring merchandise from riverboats to large ships and vice versa. By 1801, there was a formal market established in the area.

The constant military presence contributed a great deal to the economic and social development of the city. In fact, Kingston was one of the few places in Upper Canada to maintain a permanent garrison. Despite this military presence, the city's defenses and fortifications were not a high priority after 1783 and not much attention was paid to them. The outbreak of the War of 1812 proved this to be short-sighted.

The War of 1812 broke out toward the end of the Napoleonic Wars, and focused on the mounting tensions between the United States and Britain. Many American attacks were directed towards Upper Canada, because of its known loyalties to the crown. It was widely thought that Upper Canada was highly vulnerable to the American forces. By the end of the conflict in 1814, Kingston found itself a much better-protected city. Point Henry and Point Frederick were heavily fortified after the war. During the conflict, many of Upper Canada's towns were badly damaged by the Americans, but Kingston was largely untouched. This advantage, along with the increased military presence, boosted Kingston's economic and political prospects. The War of 1812 had also prompted a naval arms race between the United States and Britain. Kingston played an important role in this race, since a shipbuilding program was set up in 1813. In the end, the War of 1812 enabled the city to grow and to reposition itself as an important power in the affairs of the colony.

The War of 1812 had drawn attention to the weaknesses of the British colonies, and two major initiatives were begun to solve these problems. Firstly, authorities realized that it had been relatively easy to cut off communication between Canadian colonies by holding the banks of the St. Lawrence River. The St. Lawrence was at the time the only way to link most of the defense posts, as well as Montreal, to other communities on Lake Ontario. In 1825, a commission on the subject reported that there was a great need for an alternate waterway connection to the Great Lakes. It was Colonel John By who proposed to build a waterway from the Ottawa River via the interior lakes and the Cataraqui River to Lake Ontario. Locks were constructed along the way to overcome obstacles like rapids and waterfalls, and blockhouses were built along the way to solidify military security. The construction of the Rideau Canal was begun in 1826 and was completed in May 1832, linking Montreal to Lake Ontario by an entirely British waterway, secure from American threats.

The second shortcoming revealed during the War of 1812 was the lack of defenses at Kingston. It was clear that Kingston was a major military and economic centre for the British: it needed to be adequately protected. The main threat to the city was the prospect of a naval attack from the United States. All the same, after the War of 1812, the lake was demilitarized by joint agreement, as this was the only way to resolve disputes in the region between Britain and the United States. Thereafter, military efforts were focused on land rather than on water. In 1842, an advanced battery was constructed as an addition to Fort Henry, which overlooked the harbour, and four Martello towers were erected on Murney's Point, Market Shoal, Point Frederick and Cedar Island.

Before these fortifications were completed, Kingston, as a loyalist town, was deeply affected by several important events. Rebellions against the British crown erupted in Upper Canada and even more so in Lower Canada, involving French-Canadians, in 1837-38. Kingston did not see any direct fighting, but its garrison was sent to Lower Canada, leaving the town in the hands of the local militia and the general population. The biggest threat to Kingston itself came in November of 1838, when the Hunter's Lodge groups organized an invasion of Eastern Ontario. This invasion, along with the rebellion, was quickly suppressed in Upper Canada. In the end, Kingston played a role in the legal process, rather than providing a stage for the fighting. It was in Kingston that prisoners, considered traitors, were kept and tried.

After the Rebellions, many recommendations were made to the crown on improving the political stability of the colonies. One of these recommendations that was accepted and implemented was the union of Upper and Lower Canada into one province. The Province of Canada was officially created on the 10th of February 1841, and Kingston was chosen by the Governor General, Lord Sydenham, as the location of the new capital.

With this fortunate announcement for Kingston, thousands of politicians and government officials flocked to the town to live and work in the new seat of government. Local entrepreneurs built and rented out housing for the new habitants for a pretty profit, and inns and taverns saw throngs of new customers. Not everyone agreed with Lord Sydenham's decision. Many thought that Kingston was too small to take on such a grand role, and this proved to be true, as more and more people moved into the town. It was not able to provide the amenities required by the well-educated and well-traveled politicians that were arriving. Moreover, the town was regarded as too British for the French-Canadians and too conservative for the Reformers. The location of Kingston as the capital was also criticized because of its very close proximity to the United States and its powerful navy. Even the famous author, Charles Dickens, was unimpressed with the town when he came for a visit in 1842.

On the 19th of September 1841, Lord Sydenham died from lock-jaw following a fall from his horse, and with his death, there was no one left to defend Kingston as the capital city. Much debate followed for and against keeping the capital as Kingston, but in the end it was decided that the capital would move to Montreal. In a desperate attempt to keep the seat of government in Kingston, the locals started building an opulent city hall that would be fit for the Province's capital. Unfortunately, this gesture was not enough, and in 1843, the capital moved away for good. The town saw an exodus of government officials, and was left with large debts from its city buildings, including the large city hall. In the days following the move of the capital, some characterized Kingston as having a deserted look. The town streets were described as being constantly crowded by drunkards and prostitutes. Many "houses of ill repute" and unlicensed taverns contributed to the social problems of the city. Kingston saw terrible epidemics of cholera and typhus, which distressed the population even more.

These hard times were not the only legacy of its time as capital. Many of the large homes and distinctive buildings that were constructed during Kingston's time as the capital of Canada still remain to this day, and add considerably to the city's charm and beauty. Many of these architectural landmarks built out of the local stone give Kingston its well-known nickname: the Limestone City. Despite some social and financial problems, Kingston remained a thriving port catering to provincial commerce after the capital moved. It was in those years that Kingston evolved from being a large town to a small city. In 1846, Kingston was finally incorporated as a city and elected its first mayor, John Counter.

The end of the 19th century saw the decline of Kingston's shipping industry. More and more shipping companies found the Rideau Canal to be a less efficient waterway than the St. Lawrence, and new vessels were built that made the stop in Kingston unnecessary. Kingston saw itself being by-passed as a port city. The addition of a railway link with Toronto and Montreal would not stop its economic decline. Once the largest city in Upper Canada, by 1881, Kingston had fallen behind Toronto, Hamilton, Ottawa and London in population.

Although Kingston's trading and industrial dreams were not realized, the city managed to evolve in its own way. Kingston became the new home for many important and specialized government institutions. The town produced many influential citizens and politicians who, in turn, pushed for the expansion of the institutions that now exist in the city. Queen's University, the Royal Military College, the penitentiaries, and the hospitals are only a few of the nineteenth-century institutions that make Kingston unique.

Citizens of Kingston to this day are proud of the history of their city, and its preservation is apparent when one notices how so many elements of its past remain. From the French who first settled here, to the Loyalists, the traders and the politicians, all have served to shape the history and charm of this important city.

Bibliography

Angus, Margaret, <u>The Old Stones of Kingston: Its Buildings Before 1867</u>, Toronto: University of Toronto Press, 1966.

Armstrong, Alvin, <u>Buckskin to Broadloom: Kingston Grows Up</u>, Kingston: Kingston Whig-Standard, 1973.

"Bellevue House National Historic Site of Canada", <u>Parks Canada</u>, (December 2003):. www.pc.gc.ca

Graves, Donald E., <u>Guns Across the River: The Battle of the Windmill, 1838</u>, Toronto: The Friends of Windmill Point, 2001.

Hennesy, Peter H., Canada's Big House: The Dark History of the Kingston Penitentiary, Toronto: Dundurn Press, 1999.

<u>Historic Kingston</u>, Kingston: Kingston Historical Society.

Historic Sites and Monuments of Kingston and District, Kingston: The Kingston Whig-Standard, 1965.

Horsey, Edwin E., <u>Kingston: A century Ago</u>, Kingston: Kingston Historical Society, 1938.

Mecredy, Stephen D., <u>Fort Henry: An Illustrated History</u>, Toronto: James Lorimer & Company Ltd, 2000.

Osborne, Brian S., Donald Swainson, <u>Kingston: Building on the Past</u>, Westport: Butternut Press, 1988.

"Rockwood Asylum", SSAC Bulletin, 6-14.

Roy, James A., <u>Kingston, the King's Town</u>, Toronto: McClelland and Stewart, 1952.

The History of Kingston Psychiatric Hospital, video (2002)

Punishment Book References, X1057, George Hewell.

The Prisoner's Record, The Kingston Penitentiary, 1843-1890.

We also acknowledge the many people who agreed to be interviewed for this collection of ghost stories. We have not listed their names in the interests of their privacy, but we thank them for their many contributions.

As well, we owe a great debt to the many Archivists, Librarians, Historians and other researchers who were so generous with their time and advice. This book would not have been possible without their assistance.

Newspapers

Kingston Daily News, Kingston (Dec. 1857)

Time Out (Nov. 1990)

The Spectator (Nov. 1838, Dec. 1838, Dec. 1838, Jan. 1839)

Chronicle and Gazette (1838-1846)

Daily British Whig (1893 - 1896)

Hogben, Murray, Kingston Whig-Standard (22 Sep. 1992, 8 Oct. 1992, 17 Nov. 1992, 25 Nov. 1992)

Kingston This Week (Sep. 1992)

Kingston Whig-Standard (Apr. 1975, Sep. 1992, Apr. 1993, May 1993, May 1993, Sep. 1996)

Smyka, Mark. Kingston Whig-Standard (Sep. 1975, Nov. 1976)

Toronto Star (Feb. 1999, Apr. 2002)

Did They See A Ghost?, Kingston Daily News, Feb. 1897.

Photo Credits

p.21 Photo courtesy Queen's University Archives
(V23-ComB-Empire2)

p.25 courtesy QU Archives (V23-Dwe-Rosemount2)

p.35 Photo courtesy Fort Henry National Historic Site

p.53 Photo courtesy Queen's University Archives
(V23-RelB-Chalmers2)

p.59 courtesy QU Archives (V23-PuB-KGH-NR-1)

p.67 courtesy QU Archives (V23-Dwe-Bellevue-2)

p.75 courtesy QU Archives (V23-ComB-Prince George-3.2)

p.83 courtesy QU Archives (V23-Cem-Skeleton-1)

p.101 courtesy QU Archives (V28-P-191.2)

p.113 courtesy QU Archives (V23-MilB-MT-Cathcart-2)

This book would not have been possible without the kind assistance of the many people who agreed to be interviewed.

If you have a story of your own to share, please write to us at:

Haunted Walks Inc.
P.O. Box 1218, Stn B
Ottawa, ON K1P 5R3
Canada

info@hauntedwalk.com

If you have enjoyed this collection of ghost stories, we invite you to join us on one of our world-famous walking tours.

For more information on our year-round haunted tours of Kingston and Ottawa, please visit our website at:

www.hauntedwalk.com

Also available in 2008:

Ghosts of Ottawa
From the Files of the Haunted Walk

ISBN 1425135439
9 781425 135430